James Ellis was born in east Belfast in 1931. Son of a sheet-metal worker, he was educated at Methodist College and Queen's University, Belfast, where he read English, French and Philosophy. A Tyrone Guthrie scholarship took him to the Bristol Old Vic Theatre School. During the 1950s he worked mainly as a theatre director. His most notable production was Sam Thompson's controversial *Over the Bridge*, which was later taken on tour in Britain by Laurence Olivier's company. Best known for his work in television and film—media in which he has maintained a high profile for nearly four decades—he has also starred in West End stage productions. As a stage actor he has done seasons at the Barbican with the Royal Shakespeare Company, with the National Theatre and Sir Peter Hall's company at the Old Vic. A debut volume of poetry, *Domestic Flight*, appeared recently from Lagan Press.

By the same author

Poetry
Domestic Flight

HOME & AWAY

HOME & AWAY
Ten Tales and Three Dreams

JAMES ELLIS

LAGAN PRESS
BELFAST
2001

Published by
Lagan Press
138 University Avenue
Belfast BT7 1GZ

ISBN: 1 873687 08 7

Author: Ellis, James
Title: Home & Away:
Ten Tales and Three Dreams
2001

Cover Design: December
Set in Garamond
Printed by Noel Murphy Printing, Belfast

in memory of my mother and father

CONTENTS

Foreword

You're writing them down, Sir Walter, and now they'll be sung nae mair," said the Ettrick Shepherd's mother prophetically to Sir Walter Scott as he was compiling his epic *Minstrelsy of the Scottish Border*, thereby demonstrating that there is a price to pay for everything, including literacy.

Hitherto the balladry and folklore of that then largely remote territory had been carried in the hearts and minds of a more or less illiterate community, or rather group of communities each with a highly individual identity and proud history of its own. From then on, what had been guarded and precious was to become common knowledge on the printed page and so consequently, the collective necessity to cherish and remember it had gone for ever.

In that strictly limited sense, the innocent and perfectly natural illiteracy of childhood is an intriguing parallel. The phenomenon of an orally bilingual baby, or of an infant musical prodigy coaxing bonny tunes from his grandfather's old fiddle and not yet bogged down in the intricacies of musical notation are, I venture to suggest, not too far-fetched exempla of the workings of nature in the minefield of human progress and endeavour—man makes a machine to make an artefact, teaches others to work the machine; in time forgets how to make the artefact! All this is nothing new of course, but it is a sobering thought that *books themselves*, at least as we know them, may even now be under threat from the brave new world of computerised knowledge.

Such a development would in a way complete the circle. If in the beginning was The Word, we may be fairly certain that in the state of innocence which Christians and Jews symbolise as the *Earthly Paradise*, and other ancient civilisations referred to as an *Age of Gold*, that 'Word' was *unwritten*.

In the beginning was the Word,
And the Word was with God ...

These opening words of the Gospel According to John begin with the doctrine of the Logos or Word, which clearly makes a connection with, and underlines the influence, of Greek and Alexandrian philosophy and thought.

Where does this lead? Perhaps I am merely sifting through my own motives for putting pen to paper and reminding myself of puritanical sanctions etched into an Ulster Scots psyche —'Vanity of vanities, saith the Preacher'—

Foreword

And furthermore, my son, be admonished:
Of the making many books there is no end;
And much study is a weariness of the flesh.

Am I therefore at the expense of my mortal flesh about to yield to this temptation (*of the flesh!*) by adding to this pile of sinful pulp? Well, yes I am; but hear, I beg you, a plea in mitigation before damning me to hell or Connaught.

The story told at your mother's knee, and the nursery rhyme, or short metric story, are I submit most people's introduction to the big wide world of literature, yet both forms belong to the oral tradition—a story or tale is there to be told rather than read, and as an actor of course that is what interests me. It is also true to say that the natural transition from *telling* a tale is that 'in-between' phase, *reading aloud*, where again the histrionic element—vocal expression—comes into play. To be perfectly frank, the assembling of a group of stories of my own construction together with others translated and adapted to an idiom and background that best suits my style of delivery is in a sense, an extension of my repertoire. For the idiom and delivery I make no apology. De Maupassant's stories of everyday life, whether in a tough rural setting or in a town transfer much more readily to a provincial dialect than to any form of standardised speech; an old French teacher many years ago suggested for example that we should *think* 'North Antrim' or 'Tyrone Among the Bushes' when reading such stories as 'Le Diable' or 'La Mere Sauvage'. As for Daudet in his Provençal windmill, he was as far removed from Paris as Cushendall is from London! On that score, I have to beg the original authors' pardon for changing the settings of the stories and the names of the characters, but having taken the first liberty the second seemed inevitable—a wheen of French names scattered about the pages of tales retold for Irish ears seemed an incongruous notion. One final liberty is perhaps a little less forgivable, though it has been widely accepted in the theatre with productions of Shakespeare, and that is meddling by a few years here and there with the dates; so purists may spot the odd anachronism. I hope that the shades of Guy and Alphonse will indulge me on the grounds that a good tale is timeless.

I have to say that the cue for almost all of my presumption came from no less an authority than Monsieur Daudet himself when he more or less admitted outright that his most excellent yarn 'The Vicar of Cucugnan' (my 'Miller's Tale') had arrived virtually gift-wrapped through the post:

Annually at Candlemss, Provençal poets produce at Avignon an entertaining little booklet crammed with good

14

stories and fine verses. This year's copy has just arrived and in it I have come across an enchanting verse tale which I must translate for you, shortening it somewhat ...

So there you have it! A *fellow poet's* story, translated from Provençal into French, *retold in prose*, and *edited*—I rest my case! (the original 'author' was one, Joseph Roumanille).

This little bit of *give and take* also prompted my last item - a Romanian folktale originally in verse which I chose to retell, mainly because of its length, *alternating* between metric and prose delivery. I kept the Balkan setting but the temptation to make the builder Irish was irresistible. When I pointed out to my Romanian friend and advisor Sorina Barna that Maloney (or *Malone*) was virtually an anagram of *Manole* she laughed and gave the alternative a Balkan blessing. I also indicated, with no hint of a tongue in cheek, that the 'Irish Builder' is, and always has been, *ubiquitous*.

The man stopped and eased down his load;
and the old man said: It was here
I set my father down on this journey.

I heard this from the son of the man,
the grandson of the old man, aged himself.

Clearly, it was part of his reality;
he believed every word of it.
Yet, as he was telling me, I realised
it was no more than a variant
of the Balkan folktale."

—*from* 'The Long Bridge' by John Hewitt

Many a friendly if sometimes heated debate I had with John in days gone by over this fine point of storytelling theory. In the light of more recent experience, I would dearly love to resume the argument. Who would enlighten whom I wonder?

James Ellis
December 2000

My Uncle Julius

❖

Home And Away

Bangor, Co. Down, the pleasant seaside town just twelve miles from Belfast, has always had a certain 'genteel' air; this was certainly so in days gone by. For the Belfast working man and his family it was also, at holiday times, the most accessible of resorts. I remember from my own childhood, the famous railway slogan BANGOR AND BACK FOR A BOB—*one shilling return—unbelievable!*

Beyond that, far out in the Irish Sea, was the invisible Isle of Man, an out-of-sight and out-of-reach 'Shangri La' that might just be considered in one's wildest dreams as a possible 'once in a lifetime' holiday venue. Accessible then only by sea, the sturdy steam packet boats departed from Donegall Quay and, I believe also at one time, Bangor, revelling in such romantic names as Lady of Man, Mona's Isle *and* Ellen Vannin *(the Manx name for the Island). The Manx people, of course, with their ancient parliament, distinct native language, tasty kippers and tailless cats, were a wonder to young and old.*

A certain similarity to the genteel family portrayed in de Maupassant's tale, 'My Uncle Julius' has proved an irresistible temptation to transfer the setting from Granville on the Normandy coast with a voyage to the island of Jersey, to the little town of Bangor and the celebrated isle that is the glory of the Irish Sea.

20

My Uncle Julius

A poor old fellow with a long white beard stopped us one day in Royal Avenue and asked us if we could spare a copper. To my amazement, my friend Joe took out two shining half-crowns and gave them to the old boy—five shillings! Seeing my astonishment he said, "That poor old chap reminded me of an episode from my youth that is engraved forever on my memory. Let me tell you the whole story.

"My parents, who hailed from Bangor, were never what you'd call well off; just managing to make ends meet was about the size of it. These were the Depression years, and my father slaved long hours in a dingy office for a downright pittance. Besides myself, the only son, there were two sisters.

"My mother took our impoverished circumstances very badly, and whenever the occasion arose, did not hesitate to castigate her spouse, making hurtful remarks calculated to undermine his self-esteem. My poor father's passive response was heart-rending. He would draw an open hand across his brow as though to wipe away beads of non-existent sweat, and say nothing; his impotent martyrdom manifest for all to see, and virtually tangible.

"We economised on just about everything, and never accepted invitations to dine, for fear of having to return the compliment. We purchased life's necessities at rock-bottom prices, as oddments or ends of line; or, worse still—Tell it not in Gath—second-hand in the Belfast Variety Market. My sisters made all their own frocks, and argued interminably over the amount of braid required, which in fact cost no more than a penny a yard. Our staple diet was mainly stew—rarely champ or colcannon which were considered 'common'—and mutton, dished up in every conceivable shape and form, though nourishing, was dreadfully dull and monotonous. In addition, let it be said, mother used to create frightful scenes over lost buttons, or a rip in a pair of trousers.

"At weekends, we used to go for a stroll along the seafront, dressed in our Sunday best. My father, in an old frock-coat, bowler hat, and gloves, would offer his arm to my mother, who was decked out like a corvette on review at Spithead. My sisters, who were always ready first, would wait for the signal to depart, but at the very last moment mother was sure to discover an overlooked stain on my father's coat, and it would have to be removed on the spot with a benzine-soaked piece of rag. My father, in shirtsleeves and braces, yet still wearing his bowler, would wait stoically for the completion of this task, my mother dabbing away like the shuttle on her sewing machine, putting on her specs and removing her gloves so as not to spoil them.

"We set off, I may tell you, with some ceremony, my sisters leading the procession with arms linked; they were of marriageable age and had to be shown off on my mother's left side, whilst on her right, father put his best foot forward. I well remember the preposterous attitudes my poor parents struck on these Sunday constitutionals, their sober expressions and inflexible posture as they marched along with rhythmic gait, ramrod backs, and legs as straight as dies; as though a matter of the gravest consequence rested upon their appearance. And every Sunday, without fail, seeing the big ships enter the lough from foreign parts, my father would utter the selfsame words, 'Wouldn't it be a turn up for the books if our Julius was on board one of those.'

"Uncle Julius was my father's only brother and the family's one potential saviour, having been previously the bane of its life. It would appear he had a misspent, not to say dissolute youth; that is to say he had frittered away not only his own inheritance, but most of my father's as well. Among the well-to-do, such a character is said to 'sow his wild oats', and is what folk call indulgently a gay dog; but among the less well-off he is a downright rogue, a waster, and a black sheep. In accordance with the custom of the times, he had been packed off, steerage, on the cross-channel steamer, and thence, by banana boat, to the New World.

"He had soon set up as a dealer of some sort in New York, and promptly wrote home to the effect that he was making a few dollars, and hoped in the very near future to repay with interest the debt he owed his brother and thus make amends. His letter, coming out of the blue, created quite a stir, and Julius, who had been written off as a blackguard, was immediately back in favour as a right decent sort, with the proverbial heart of corn—a true Davenport and fine upstanding stalwart of that respected and worthy family. The skipper of one transatlantic vessel told us he had leased a large store and was doing excellent business.

"Two years afterwards a second letter arrived, stating, 'My dear Philip, I am writing to tell you that I am in good health, and business is good also. I am setting off tomorrow on a long trip to South America, and may be out of touch for several years. If I don't write in the meantime, don't fret, for once I have made my fortune I shall return to Belfast and thence to dear old Bangor where I hope we shall live happily together in style and comfort.'

"This letter, as you can imagine, became a sort of family testament, and was taken out on the slightest pretext and read aloud to all and sundry.

"Ten years went by and nothing more was heard from Uncle Julius, but somehow, as time went by, father's expectations seemed to rise if anything and even mother was fond of remarking: 'When Julius comes home it will be a different kettle of fish; there's a man who knows how to prosper in life!' And every Sunday, watching the big black liners entering the lough, the old man would murmur the perpetual prayer, 'Wouldn't it be a turn-up for the books ...' and so on. So much of a ritual had this become that we could almost visualise the bold Julius waving a handkerchief and calling out: 'Hi there, Philip!' Countless daydreams rested on this grand homecoming. We were going to purchase a little stone house in the Mournes with my uncle's money, near Rostrevor. In fact its theme was so recurrent, that I began to believe my father might actually have put down a small deposit.

"My elder sister was 28 at this time, and the younger was 26; neither had yet found a husband, and that was a cause for concern. At last, however, a suitor materialised for the younger one—a clerk, not moneyed, but presentable looking. I always maintained that Uncle Julius' letter, brought out and shown to him at a crucial moment, probably tipped the scales. He was immediately snapped up, and it was decided there and then, that after the wedding the entire family would go on a trip to the Isle of Man.

"The Isle of Man is the ideal resort for the not so well-off. It is no great distance, yet a short sea voyage takes you virtually onto foreign soil; for the Manx people are very different from the rest of us, and they even have their own parliament, the Tynwald, far more ancient than Westminster. So, for the price of this short sea trip, one has the opportunity to study at close quarters the customs and manners of a completely foreign people who, at the same time, enjoy the privilege and protection of the Union Jack. This trip became our obsession, our sole expectation, and all-consuming object of our hopes and dreams.

"At last the great day came. I can picture it all as though it were yesterday—the ship building up a head of steam beside the pier, my father fussing over the handling of our three bits of baggage; my mother nervously gripping the arm of her unmarried daughter, who seemed quite bewildered since her sister's departure, like a chick abandoned by the rest of her brood; and lastly the bride and groom who always loitered at the rear, as I constantly turned round to look for them.

"A blast on the whistle—by now we were aboard— and the vessel pulled away, heading out for a sea that was as flat and green as a slab of Connemara marble. We passed the Copelands and watched the Irish coast vanish into the distance, naively proud and thrilled, like those unused to travel. My father's corporation protruded from his unfastened coat, which had been meticulously cleaned that very morning, and which exuded in a wide arc that odour of benzine which I always associated with Sundays.

"Presently, father spied two fashionably dressed dames whose escorts were treating them to oysters. An elderly mariner, virtually in rags, was prising them apart with a stubby knife and handing them to the gentlemen, who in turns passed them to the ladies. They were partaking of the treat most fastidiously, grasping the shells in fine lawn handkerchiefs and tilting their heads forwards so as not to spoil their frocks; finally drinking the liquid with a dainty sip, before tossing the shells over the ship's rail.

"No doubt my father was duly impressed by the concept of eating oysters on shipboard; as like as not he looked upon the custom as a sure sign of class. Going back to my mother and sisters he asked causally: 'Would you like me to treat you to a few oysters?' Mother hesitated, no doubt on the grounds of expense, but my sisters accepted at once, whilst she, in querulous tones added, 'They upset my digestion; get some for the children, by all means, but not too many lest they should be sick. None for Joseph though—boys should not be mollycoddled.' I regarded the girls' preferment as downright unjust, but made no protest, staying behind and watching with envy as my father rather pompously propelled the two girls and his son-in-law towards the ragged mariner. The other party had moved away, and my father at once began to tell my sisters how to eat the molluscs without spilling the juice. He grabbed one in order to demonstrate, and in trying to imitate the actions of the fine ladies, spilled it over his coat. Mother audibly commented, 'That's what comes of showing off!'

"Suddenly my father looked taken aback, recoiling several paces and staring fixedly at his little brood gathered round the oyster seller; then abruptly he came towards us and said in a whisper to my mother: 'It's uncanny how much that fellow looks like Julius?'

"'Julius? What Julius?'

"'My brother, of course. He's the living spit! If I didn't know he was prospering in the New World, I'd swear it was him!'

"'You're crazy,' my mother said. 'Since you know for certain it can't be him, what makes you say such a thing?' But father persisted, 'Take a look for yourself, Clara. I'd be glad of your opinion.'

"She went to join her daughters. I too ran across

and stared. He was old and scruffy with a wizened face and he did not glance up from his work. Mother hurried back straight away. I noticed she was shaking.

"'I do believe it's him,' she said, 'but ask the captain about him; and do be careful what you say. We don't want that toe-rag on our doorstep again.'

"Father strode off and this time I followed him. The master of the ship, a tall lean man with sandy-coloured sideburns, was striding back and forth on his bridge as though he were the commander of the mail boat to India. My father approached him decorously, beating about the bush and larding his questions with compliments: 'How big was the island, sir? What were its chief products, its population and regional customs? What was the nature of the soil, captain?' And so on, and so on—one would have thought he was enquiring about the United States of America at the very least. Finally the talk turned to the excellent vessel we were travelling on—the *S.S. Lady of Man*, and of course, her crew. At long last, in a thin voice, he enquired about the elderly mariner. The captain, who was tiring of the conversation replied rather shortly: 'He's an old tramp I picked up last year in the States and brought back to the United Kingdom. I gather he has relatives in Bangor; but he doesn't want to show himself because he owes them money. His name is Julius. Julius Davenport, or Devonport—something like that. It appears he was well-off for a while over there, but the Depression put paid to all that, and you can see what he has come to now—'Buddy can you spare a dime and all that jazz'—My father turned a deathly pale and muttered in a hoarse voice, 'Ah yes! Of course. I'm not at all surprised ... thank you very much.' And he wandered off as the rather puzzled captain followed him with his gaze.

"He returned looking so devastated that my mother said uneasily: 'Do sit down, Philip, or people will wonder what's the matter.' He subsided onto a bench, breathless and virtually incoherent, 'It's ... it's him all right. What ... what are we going to do?'

"'Pull yourself together,' she replied sharply. 'We must rescue the children for a start; since Joseph already knows the truth, he can take care of that. Whatever transpires, we must make sure our son-in-law remains in ignorance.' My poor father seemed to have gone to pieces. All he could do was murmur over and over, 'What a disaster ... what a disaster.' Mother launched into one of her famous tantrums, 'I always thought that swindler would come to a sticky end! What else could you expect from a Davenport!'

"And my father drew his hand across his brow as he always did when his wife began her deprecations. 'Give Joseph some change so he can pay for the oysters. What a spectacle it would make to be recognised by that tramp! Let's retire to the farthest end of the ship to ensure he comes nowhere near us.' Leaving me with a ten shilling note, they sallied off— father forlorn, mother in high dudgeon.

"My sisters looked surprised when I showed up. I said the sea swell had made mother queasy, and I asked the oyster man how much we owed him—I felt like calling him uncle, but instead I said mister. 'Two shillings and sixpence,' he replied. I held out the note and he gave me change.

"I looked at his hand—a poor, gnarled, weather-beaten hand—and I gazed on the face—an unhappy, careworn old countenance—and I solemnly said to myself: 'This is my uncle, my father's brother, my uncle!' I gave him a sixpenny tip and he said, 'God bless you, young sir.' His tone was that of a beggar who had been given an alms, and I couldn't help wondering if he had begged over there, across the broad Atlantic: *"Buddy, can you spare a dime ..."*

"My sisters stared open-mouthed, amazed by my generous gesture. When I returned the seven shillings to my father, my mother demanded sternly: 'Was that three shillings worth? It's not possible!' I responded in a steady voice: 'I gave the gentleman a sixpenny tip.' My mother let out a gasp, and staring me straight in the face, said: 'You're off your head giving a sixpence to that ... that tramp!' A quick glance from my father stopped her in her tracks as he nodded towards their son-in-law, then everyone fell silent.

"Ahead of us, on the horizon, a purple shadow loomed above the surface of the sea—it was the Isle of Man. As we neared the harbour I was consumed with an intense desire to see my Uncle Julius one more time, to rush up and say something affectionate and conciliatory, but as no-one was requiring oysters, he had vanished, probably down the foul-smelling hold which now served as his home.

"We returned by the Belfast boat so as not to run into him again. My mother was weighed down by anxiety. I never saw my father's brother again.

"And that, my friend, is why you will sometimes catch me giving a five shilling donation to a tramp."

The Miller's Tale

❖

Alphonse Daudet (1840–1897), the celebrated Provençal storyteller and author of Lettres de Mon Moulin *(Letters from My Mill), is the source of my next tale. It concerns the parish priest of a fictitious town called Cucugnan. Daudet himself makes several modest disclaimers, asserting firstly that he had merely abridged and adapted it from a tale in a booklet produced by his fellow bards in the town of Avignon; then attributing the authorship to one Joseph Roumanville who, in turn, he says, had it from another fellow and so on.*

The 'moral' is of universal appeal and since my great grandfather ground flour at Cushendall in County Antrim, where the nearby Lammas Fair was a noted rendezvous for spinners of yarns and singers of songs, I have taken the liberty of becoming another link in the chain that makes a tall tale taller still!

The bones of the plot remain intact but the northern locality is a far cry from Daudet's sun-baked Provence and I have added an Orwellian touch to the extra-terrestrial characters that the original author, or authors, could only have dreamt of; but stay awake, for you might miss it!

Joseph Miller was, as a matter of fact, my great-grandfather's real name and he was, in the mid-part of

The Miller's Tale

the 19th century, the incumbent of the mill at Cushendall, which is just about right for chronology. His impressive address, proudly recalled by mother was:

Joseph Miller,
Miller,
The Mill,
Cushendall.

and a substantial relic of the old establishment remains intact, tucked away behind a modern house in the town. I like to imagine it retold by my great-grandfather to friends and cronies over a jug of hot Bushmills whiskey on a cold winter's night round a roaring turf fire. Perhaps he picked up his version from a tinker or a pedlar. In the good old days, a tale might wander far and wide, crossing boundaries as readily as herds of buffalo, or droves of migrating swallows.

An Explanatory Note

One glaring 'anachronism' in this tale that may cause M. Daudet to turn in his grave and which good Father Martin may well have considered a diabolical liberty, is the introduction of computer technology to the heavenly sphere. Of course it will be unforgivable to purists, and who would blame them! I merely offer a few words of explanation for my eccentric impulse.

Firstly, the faux pas occurs in a Dream Sequence, and dreams are, even by dictionary definition, arguably prophetic. Secondly, I see no cogent reason, for the true believer, to keep Paradise for ever walled up in some archaic time warp. Of course any such ineffable realm must be light years ahead of our poor fallen planet, and a modest prediction that such might be the case would not I hope have been beyond the narrative capabilities of my Victorian great grandfather. Alright, so it hadn't occurred to Daudet—what the hell! I myself, as a child, found the idea of a recording angel at a big desk writing out all the sins of the world in longhand into a big ledger, nothing short of far-fetched, and at one time suggested sending him a typewriter for Christmas! I think I've said enough to damn myself to eternal perdition in the eyes of honest translators so I will say no more ...

The Miller's Tale

Father Martin was the parish priest of ... I was going to say Cushendall, but that would be unfair to the good folk of that fine town, who are proverbial for their piety and regular attendance at church and chapel; so for the sake of discretion and 'oul' dacency', shall we say—

Father Martin was the parish priest of Ballyslapgattery. Here was a man of infinite goodness and humility, who loved his parish and adored his erring flock, as a father will dote on his children, however wayward. In his humble opinion 'Ballyslap' would have been 'heaven on earth' if only that flock would enter the sheepfold, but, unfortunate pastor that he was, he couldn't even get them as far as the shedding ring—the confessional was so neglected it was roofed over by a tracery of cobwebs! As for the holy days of Lent, the host as often as not, remained unconsecrated in the golden cup.

Poor Father Martin, sick at heart and feeling a miserable failure at his chosen vocation, prayed continually to God for guidance—all, it seemed, to no avail. Then one day, sitting alone in the sacristy, he watched a spider struggling to span what seemed an unbridgeable gap in the vaulted ceiling, and he remembered the grand story of King Robert the Bruce alone in the cave on nearby Rathlin Island; did not the king learn from the spider's determination to 'Try, try, and try again', and did he not return to Scotland, claim the throne, and defeat the English at the Battle of Bannockburn! That did it—the good man went down on his knees one more time and prayed as he had never prayed before—and this time God heard him, as you shall see; but first he felt impelled, or was 'inspired' to put up a big notice in the square on market day which read as follows:

To the Good People of Ballyslapgattery
and surrounding districts

If you attend Mass this coming Sunday you will hear something greatly to your advantage. This concerns every family in the parish without exception and entails the presence of every member of each family, save only the aged and infirm. The information you will receive will be of benefit only at first hand; hearsay will not be worth a brass farthing.

Perhaps it was the mention of the farthing, and the hint of cash benefits, that drew the biggest crowd the parish had ever known—it was packed to the roof! Perhaps God was just moving in that mysterious way of His, these wonders to perform; whatever way you look at it, good Father Martin had a captive audience.

Now it is customary for the priest, before reading the gospel, to make the sign of the triple cross; but some eyewitnesses swear that he did it again after the gospel reading, just before ascending the pulpit. For those of you who are ignorant of these matters, the triple cross is made by imprinting the thumb on the forehead, lips, and chest, and when the priest does it, the people follow suit. Its significance is that the word may penetrate the mind, be spoken by the lips, and remain in the heart— very sound psychology! 'Read, learn, and inwardly digest.' Father Martin began:

"Dear children of God, whether you believe what I am about to tell you or not, is entirely a matter for your own conscience; but as you all know, I am not a man given to vain fancies or wishful thinking. Just the other night—to be exact, the night before I put up that notice in the market square, I found myself standing outside some shining gates—not the ones to Major Turnkey's big house outside the town—no, dear friends, I am talking about the Pearly Gates—oh yes, the gates of Paradise! Well, I knocked, and Saint Peter himself answered, 'Lord bless us and save us,' says he, 'if it isn't Father Martin! And what brings you here ahead of your time? What can I do for you?'

"'Your Holiness,' says I, forgetting in the heat of the moment that he was no longer 'of this world', 'you are the keeper of the Great Book—can you tell me, if it's not an impertinence, how many of the good people of Ballyslapgattery do you have here in Paradise?'

"'Come in. Come in. How can I refuse you?' said the big man. 'Sit down and take the weight off your legs and we'll look into it together; though you're a bit out of date with your 'Great Book', Father—we have it all down on a big screen these days. Oh, we've had this installed for centuries now, but you'll not see its like on earth till near the end of your millennium.' At that, the screen lit up, and it was brighter than the Book of Kells, or the sea of Moyle on a fine summer's evening.

"Peter put his specs on and began pressing switches—

'Now, then ... B. Bally, Bally, Bally—there's an awful lot of Ballies—'

"'That's because—' said I helpfully.

"'I know,' said Peter, 'it's Irish for place, or town of ... Ballybunion, Ballyclare, Ballymena ... Ballysaggart! Now, that 'the town of the priest'—oh, he knows his onions, does Peter. 'Not a thing, Father; a blank screen. Not one sinner—no more than you'd find a fishbone in a turkey carcass.'

"'What!' said I, 'No-one? Not one soul? It's not possible!'

"'See for yourself,' says Peter, 'if you think I'm pulling your leg.'

"'It's no laughing matter,' says I, wringing my hands and jumping up and down, 'Lord have mercy on us all,' I cried, but the good Saint Peter did his best to calm me.

"'Now don't upset yourself or you'll have a stroke, it's clearly not your fault. They are probably doing their wee spell in Purgatory.'

"'Oh, good kind Saint Peter,' said I, 'for the love of God allow me to go there and console them.'

"'By all means,' said the former Holy Father, 'but slip on these Doc Martens, for the tracks there aren't all they should be ... that's the stuff! Now follow that path

straight forenenst you, and when you get to the foot of
the brae, there's a turning. On your right you'll see a
silver door, decorated all over with black crosses. 'Knock
and it shall be opened unto you', as it says somewhere in
the scriptures. God be with you and keep your chin up!'

"Well I followed that path as best I could, and I kept
on following it right to the bitter end—what a
nightmare! Well, it would have been, only this was for
real. That narrow path, that got narrower and narrower,
was choked with whins and thistles, thorns and briars,
infested with poisonous toads, and snakes that hissed
and spat—as you know, there are no snakes in Ireland,
so this was, as sure as hell, an out-of-body experience! At
last I reached the silver door and knocked.

"'Who's there?' a dolorous, gravelly voice enquired.

"'The parish priest of Ballyslapgattery,' I replied.

"'Bally ...?'

"'—Slapgattery,' said I, boldly.

"'Enter,' said the voice, and so I entered.

"A tall, handsome angel with wings as dark as a
midwinter's night, and a robe as bright as the fairest day,
with a key slung from his waist encrusted with precious
stones, was writing names in the biggest black book you
ever saw. Scratch, scratch, went the pen, scratch, scratch.

"'You'll have to excuse me,' said the angel. 'There is such a backlog here, we enter the names in the book first, and then transfer them to the celestial 'internet'. Now, what is the purpose of your visit?'

"'Most reverend angel of God. I should like very much to know—tell me if I am being presumptuous— have you any souls here from the parish of Ballyslapgattery? I am their humble priest, you see.'

"'Souls from Bally ...?'

"'—Slapgattery, your worship.'

"'Are you ... Father Martin?'

"'Your humble servant, holy angel.'

"The angel wet his fingers and leafed through the book, 'Nothing here,' said he with a sigh, then turned to the giant screen. A flick of a switch, then a blinding light, and a sorrowful shake of the head.

"'I must inform you, Father Martin, there is not a soul from Ballyslapgattery in all of Purgatory.'

"'Not one sinner! Oh, Jesus, Mary, and Joseph, then where in heaven's name can they be?'

"'Dear servant of God, they must be in Paradise then. Where in hell else would you expect them to be?'

"'But ... but ... esteemed angel of the Almighty, I have just come from there.'

"'And?'

"'They are not there either, Holy One.'

"'Well, Father, if they are not in Paradise, and not in Purgatory, you're going to have to face it ...'

"'Oh, no, not that! I couldn't bear it! It's not possible ... perhaps Saint Peter wasn't telling the truth. Perhaps he was telling fibs—he has been known to—oh, God forgive me, of course he wasn't, the cock didn't crow ... what am I saying! What poor miserable sinners we all are—how can I be happy in heaven without my flock?'

"'My dear father Martin, since you insist on seeing the worst with your own two eyes, you must take the downward path; and my advice to you is to run all the way to the bottom, without stopping if you can manage it; don't let your feet touch the ground. At the bottom of the hill, on your left, you will see a huge gate, and all will be revealed ... and may your God go with you,' he added cryptically, giving me an old-fashioned look as he firmly closed the door.

"It was a long, steep boreen, strewn with glowing coals from top to bottom, and slippery as hell. I staggered down uncertainly as though I'd been on the bottle, stumbling every step of the way and drenched in perspiration—the sweat pouring off me in cobs as we say—I was short of breath and my throat was parched with the drouth; but miraculously my feet were not scorched, thanks to the Doc Martens good Saint Peter had lent me.

"When I had hirpled and hobbled, skated and skidded to a standstill, I glanced to my left, and saw ... not a door, but a yawning cleft, like the jaws of a mighty oven! Oh, dear brothers and sisters, what an awesome sight it was! There, no-one asks your name. There, no records are kept, no roll-call of who is who. There, dear people, the portal is open wide, and sinners enter in droves, just as they do in the pubs and dance halls on a continental Sunday—never having come near Mass or confession—I was dripping gobbets of sweat, yet shivering with the cold; my teeth were chattering, my hair was standing on end, and I smelt the horrible stench of burning flesh, like when the blacksmith scorches the hoof of a frisky mare before he shoes her. I was gasping for breath in that airless, stifling heat; I could hear the most horrible shrieks and lamentations—loud wailing, cries of pain, and loathsome threats and curses—

"'Are yis comin' in or not?' asked an ugly divel with horns the size of a highland heifer, prodding me playfully with his pitchfork.

"'Indeed I'm not,' says I, 'I'm a friend of God.'

"'A friend of God!' says he, with a great guffaw. 'Well, what are you wantin' here, ye mangy oul' crow?'

"'I'm here, I'm here ...' says I, in a feeble voice— 'Could you give me a moment to catch my breath; I've come a long way, I can hardly stand, I can barely ... oh, dear oh, dear—could you tell me if, by any chance ...'

"'Spit it out, man! Spit it out!'

"'Have you anyone here from Ballyslapgattery?'

"The divel stared in utter disbelief, slack-jawed and snarling ...

"'Are you trying to take a rise out of me, mister? Don't you know very well the whole of Slapgattery is here— every last sinner! Look over there, 'Monsignor Godsbody', and behold what we do with the Ballyslap crowd'—and I saw with these old eyes, enveloped in searing sheets of flame —

"That clown, Buck Geragthy—you all remember him—getting blind drunk then beating up the wife; till she lost her eye and split his skull with a soup ladle. I saw doe-eyed Dervla—'butter wouldn't melt'—lying on her back on a red hot haystack! Dan O'Rawe, who made his fires from his neighbours' turf stacks, buried to the neck in white-hot ash—Biddy the gleaner who stole great bags of barley, McAllister the tipstaff who took bribes at the Assizes, Paudge Dougherty who overcharged for water from his well, and that snob Telfer who looked the other way when I hurried to take the sacraments to the dying—much good it did them—each, and every one of them roasting in Hell! Need I go on?

"You are convinced by now, I'm sure," continued Father Martin, "that this cannot continue; I am charged with the welfare of your souls and I must, indeed I insist on saving you from that abyss into which you are all about to plunge, headlong, and for all eternity. Tomorrow I shall set about my task, and what a task it will be! How shall I tackle it? To accomplish it thoroughly, each step will have to be undertaken and conducted in an orderly fashion. I will engage one row at a time, which is the usual practice at a properly organised céilídh, or when you go dancing at the cross-roads. Here is my plan.

"First thing tomorrow, I shall hear the confessions of the elderly—male and female; that shouldn't take long—on Tuesday, the infants; that is a formality. On Wednesday, I'll hear the girls and boys over the age of seven—that could take all day! "Bring up the child ..."

and so on ... on Thursday, I shall await the men—we'll make that as brief as possible—and on Friday, the women—I'll say it now, ladies, 'Don't get too long-winded!' That leaves Saturday—ah, yes, the miller—he'll need the whole day to himself—now, where was I? Oh, Sunday, of course! Well, let's hope we've completed the entire labour by Sunday, when I shall see you all at Mass, healthy and sound in mind and body, and at peace with your Maker, and our Saviour, Jesus Christ. You see, dear children, 'there is a time and a season.' When the corn is ripe, it must be cut; when the grain's distilled, it must be drunk; and when there is dirty linen, it must be washed, and washed thoroughly. That, by God's grace, is what I wish for you. Amen."

The wish was father to the thought, and what was thought was done. The linen was washed, and came out as white as snow. And ever since that unforgettable Sunday, and the momentous week that followed, the sweet perfume of virtuous, clean-living Cush—oops! Beg pardon—of shining, sinless Slapgattery has purified the air for miles around; and the good shepherd Martin, carefree and blithe of heart, basks in the sure and certain hope of everlasting bliss for himself and his snow-white flock. In fact, only the other night, he dreamt ...

That grasping his shepherd's crook, and followed in joyful procession by the entire village—bathed in celestial light and the odour of sanctity; flanked by fresh faced choirboys chanting the *Te Deum*—he was ascending the heavenly way, to join the multitude of saints in the beautiful city of God.

There you have it! Great-grandfather Miller's fireside yarn picked up from a travelling bard at the Lammas Fair.

The Hidey-Hole

Home And Away

This story of de Maupassant is transferred from the River Seine, near Paris, to the River Lagan and a Belfast suburb, Stranmillis, where nowadays a smart restaurant is situated by the waterside, near where Molly Ward's lock used to be and the old horse trams came to a halt. It was a favourite childhood haunt, especially at weekends, and horse-drawn barges still passed through on their way to Lambeg, Lisburn and beyond. Between there and the Minnowburn at Shaw's Bridge, fishermen lined the banks, men walked their dogs and courting couples kept their trysts. Molly Ward's old shebeen, the haunt of bargees and their doxies, moonshiners with their 'mountain dew' and anglers in search of a drop of the hard stuff, had disappeared by then, but was still fresh in the memory of my parents, uncles and aunts.

The Hidey-Hole

Blows and wounds occasioning death, in other words manslaughter—this was the charge that lead to the appearance in court of Leo Fox, upholsterer. As well as the defendant, there were principal witnesses: the widow Fleming, relict of the deceased, and the men—Louis Laidlaw, journeyman cabinet-maker, and John Durden, plumber. Near the accused sat his wife: small, ugly, and looking rather like a monkey dressed in women's clothes.

Here is how Fox (Leopold), recounted the affair in his own words.

"Afore God, it was a misfortune of which I was at all times a prime victim, and through no fault of my own. The facts will speak for themselves, your lordship. I am an honest man, a tradesman, an upholsterer in the same street for some sixteen years; known, liked, respected and highly regarded by all, as my neighbours will testify ... I like work, I like thrift, I like honest folk and honest pastimes. That has been my downfall, more's the pity; but my spirit is unbowed and I still value my self-respect.

"Well then, every Sunday, my wife, whom you see, and myself, have, for the past five years, spent the entire day on the Lagan, near Shaw's Bridge. We go there for the good fresh air of course, but above all, we go for the fishing. Now, that particular pastime your honour—fishing with rod and line—we love to distraction, as other folk are hooked on scallions, or pickled onions! It is Millie who has nagged me into this obsession, who gets more carried away than I do—a holy terror, in fact—and all the grief arising from this affair stems from her, as you shall see in due course.

"Me, I am the strong silent type, not prone to argy-bargying at the drop of a hat—but her! Oh dear, oh dear, oh dear! She's not much to look at; she's small, she's skinny, but oh boy, is she vicious. A right wee vixen, if you'll pardon the pun, your honour—I mean, with my name being Fox, if you get my meaning—but then, there is no denying her good qualities. She has them in abundance, and very useful they are too, in the way of business; but her temper! Ask around, your worship. Day in, day out, she upbraids me for my good nature—Why do I put up with this? Why do I put up with that? Why don't I stand up for myself?—If I listened to her, your lordship, I would have at least three fist fights a month."

Mrs. Fox ventured to interrupt, "Oh, that's right, make a show of us; but he who laughs last, laughs longest; it's always the case."

The accused, turning to his spouse with some warmth, responded, "Well, this is my case, dear, and I'll say what I like, when I like, and where I like—were the case yours, you'd be laughing on the wrong side of your face by now.

"To continue, your honour: Every Saturday evening as regular as clockwork we would head out for Molly Ward's lock to be ready to fish from the crack of dawn on the day following. The routine had become second nature you might say. Some distance upstream, where the Minnowburn flows into the main river—near to Shaw's Bridge, as I've already stated—I discovered, some three years ago now, a wee 'hidey-hole', if you understand me—and what a hidey-hole your honour! You've never seen the like of it—a shady nook beneath the trees, and at your feet a pool, a hidden pool; eight feet of water, maybe ten, with subterranean channels under the bank; a right nest of fishes, a very paradise for a fisherman. That pool, your worship, I considered to be my very own, seeing as how I was, so to speak, its very own Christopher Columbus. Everyone on the river acknowledges that, your honour, everyone, without question. People say, 'That is Fox's Hidey Hole,' and there's an end of it; no-one comes near it ...

"Sure of my ground then, I return there regularly as the proprietor, or colonist. Arriving on a Saturday, the wife and I will jump into *Delilah* and cast off— *Delilah* is the name of the little skiff I had made especially at the Annadale Boatyard; light and manoeuvrable, she is—and off we go to lay bait. As for bait, I'm your only man, as all my colleagues will tell you. You ask me what bait I use? I cannot answer that; no disrespect, but it is private; and besides, it has no bearing on the case. A hundred times and more I've been asked that question; I've been offered gifts of moonshine, jellied eels, and fried fish suppers to loosen my tongue, but never have I divulged. 'Where do they spring from, these fat chub of yours?' they ask me slyly, offering enticements to winkle out my recipe, but only my wife shares that secret and she would no more give it away than I would. Isn't that right, Millie, dear?"

The judge intervened to say: "Would you get to the point as quickly as possible," and the accused replied: "I'm coming to it. I'm coming to it.

"On Saturday, 8th July then, alighting from the Stranmillis tram at around 5.30 in the afternoon, we set off to lay bait as usual. The weather looked settled and I said to Millie as we came back down, 'It's set fair for tomorrow, my love,' and she replied, 'It's promising, yes.' We said little else of any consequence.

"After a wee picnic by the lockside, I was happy and contented and looking forward to the morrow; but facing across, as we were, to Molly Ward's shebeen, I felt a sudden drouth come over me—that was the taper that lit the fuse, your worship, that was the squib that blew up in our faces the following day— says I to Millie, 'It's a fine summer's evening, dear; sure a wee drop of the cratur' wouldn't come amiss— just a wee nightcap, that's all'. Well, your honour, as I'm sure you know yourself, if you get it just right, you sleep like a top, but a drop too much, and it keeps you awake all night! To be fair, the wife had warned me—

I'll always give credit where credit is due—'You'll please yourself, I know,' says she, 'but you could poleaxe yourself and not be fit to rise tomorrow!' It was true, it was wise, it was prudent I confess, but I was bloody minded, and insisted on my precious carry-out in the face of common sense.

"Well, wouldn't you know, I went and overdid it—two o'clock in the morning and I still hadn't got off to sleep, so I topped the dose up for the umpteenth time—that did it! In the middle of a rousing chorus of 'My Darlin' Little Cruiskeen Lawn', the moonshine struck—out like a light, your worship! The Archangel Gabriel blowing the last trumpet would not have roused me; though Millie did, eventually, at well after six. I gave myself a cat's lick, threw on my jersey and leggin's, and got to the boat somehow, Millie trailing after me, her wee short legs pumping like pistons. We scrambled into the skiff, somehow, and rowed furiously upstream—Too late! Too late! My place was usurped! I was gobsmacked—never before had such a thing occurred, your honour, never once in three whole years. I felt as though daylight robbery had taken place before my very eyes; I felt unmanned, humiliated, and for once was all but speechless, babbling incoherently, and mostly to myself. Meanwhile, the wife laid straight into me, 'You and your nightcap! Well then, you drunken sot, you pot-bellied soak, are you satisfied now, you fat pig?' I said not one word, your honour. It was well-deserved, and fair comment under the circumstances. I disembarked silently and tried to make the best of things. Perhaps he'd fail to get a bite, and clear off, this character.

"He was a skinny little beggar in Oxford bags and white boater—what my grandfather would have called 'a wee sparleyfart'. He had a fat wife who sat just behind him doing her needlework. When she saw us pulling up nearby, she muttered under her breath, 'Is there no other spot on the river, for heaven's sake!' and Millie, who was seething, responded, 'Respectably brought up people would ask what the form is, before ensconcing themselves in other folk's places that's already spoken for.' 'Houl' your wheest, Millie', says I, for I didn't want trouble. 'Let's just wait and see what transpires.'

"By now, we had moored *Delilah* under the willows, and at this point me and her were fishing cheek by jowl with the other two—at this juncture, your worship, I have to go into some detail ...

"We'd not been there five minutes when the wee skitter's float starts bobbin' up and down like a yo-yo, and he hauls in a chub as thick as my thigh; well, maybe not quite, but a whopper just the same. I'm sweating profusely, and the heart is banging away like a Lambeg drum; meanwhile Millie is muttering audibly through pursed lips, 'Get an eyeful of that, ye glipe!'

"Just then Mr. Bunting, the grocer at Edenderry—who fishes for gudgeon by inclination—waves from his passing rowing boat and yells, 'I see someone has hijacked your territory, Mr. Fox.'

"'Too right,' I yell back, 'but some people have no grasp of etiquette or local rules.'

"The wee sparleyfart let on he hadn't heard—likewise his great fat slob of a wife, the ugly cow—"

"Watch your language," the judge interjected, "Your choice of words is offensive to the deceased's widow."

"I'm sorry, your honour," said Fox, "My emotions got the better of me.

"Anyway, in no time at all, Mr. Sparley lands another chub, then a third, a fourth, all in the space of about twenty minutes. Well, the tears just welled up in me your honour, and I could sense Mrs. Fox coming steadily to the boil—she went on at me nonstop, and that's a fact—'I've seen nothing to beat this,' says she. 'You do realise it's your fish he's knocking off, don't you, and you sat there on your fat arse not fit to catch cold, or even a tadpole; oh, it makes my skin crawl, just to think of it!'

"Unruffled, I kept repeating to myself over and over, 'Just last out till dinner time and he'll pack up and go for a meal.' You see, your honour, we don't take a dinner break, we bring a packed lunch with us on the skiff and have it on the river bank. Well, blow me, it strikes midday, and doesn't Mrs. Sparley ...

"Fleming," the judge interjected, "Mrs. Fleming— widow of the deceased—"

"Aye, well, anyway ... " continued Fox, undeterred, "she only produces a cooked chicken wrapped in newspaper, and while the two of them are munching away doesn't he go and land another chub. Millie and me, more gloomy than ever, toyed with our modest fare, but our hearts weren't in it.

"Normally, at this time, I get out the old *Ireland's Saturday Night*—you know, the sports paper that has that column in it by Mrs. McNiece—she slays me, that woman, some of the things she comes out with! I like to wind my Millie up by pretending I know her personally, but of course that's not true; I've never clapped eyes on her. It gets on her goat just the same! On the day in question, however, she flew clean off the handle, so I clammed up straight away. Just then, our two witnesses, Messrs. Laidlaw and Durden showed up on the far bank, and the sparleyfart recommenced casting, hauling his catches in by the minute, while I raised not so much as a tickle.

"'I say, darling,' the fat one chips in, 'This place is really idyllic, we must come here always.'

"I felt a numbing chill in the small of my back, and Mrs. Fox kept up her constant barrage of abuse, 'Call yourself a man! Chicken's blood, that's what flows in your veins!'

"By then I was at cracking point, your worship, so I says, 'I think I'd better go before I do something I'll regret.'

"Well, just as though she were dangling a red hot poker under my nose, she hisses spitefully under her breath, 'Oh that's right, Yellow Belly—Fly the field, and leave our precious hidey-hole to them 'uns ... ' adding malevolently, by way of twisting the knife, and raising her voice to fever pitch, 'Go on then, Chicken-liver—Run, King James, run!'

"She was referring of course, my lord, to the annual mock Battle at Scarva, which commemorates King William's victory at the Battle of the Boyne. Well I myself, being true blue and loyal orange to the core— I'd ask the court to take note of that—was cut to the quick, as you can imagine; and thereafter never budged—'Not an inch!' as I'm sure the witnesses will testify.

"My reward for that was to be rooted to the spot while your man lands the prize catch of the day—a great big freshwater bream—never did I see such a fish! Never! Well at the sight of this, Mrs. Fox raised the pitch of her decibels by a full octave, voicing her anguish in a shrill falsetto, 'Now see what they're up to—that's downright theft—since it's us that laid the bait, the very least they can do is pay our expenses, in full!'

"At that, unable any longer to ignore the onslaught, the sparleyfart's wife pipes up in challenging tones, 'Is it us you are addressing, by any chance?'

"'I am addressing fish thieves who profit from funds invested by others.'

"'Is it us you are calling fish thieves, may one ask?'

"'If the cap fits ...'

"... and so on, and so on ... thus it fell to a war of words, and thence to pushing and shoving. They shouted and bawled, and screamed and squawked to such an extent that our two witnesses on the opposite bank cried out in jest, 'Keep the noise down, ladies, you're disturbing your husbands' peace!'

"The fact of the matter is, my lord—and I speak on oath and in solemn respect for the memory of the dead man—myself and the little sparleyfart sat motionless as tree-stumps, neither moving a muscle. We stayed put, our two noses pointing at the water as though we heard nothing; but, bless us and save us, did we or did we not catch an earful, 'You're nothing but a liar!' 'You're nothing but a slag!' 'You're a slut, you're a trollop, you're a whoor, you're a hussy!' and they cursed and they swore like sailors on shore leave.

"Suddenly I heard a whacking noise behind me, and turned round, involuntarily, your worship. It was the fat one setting about my wife with an umbrella: *Bash! Bash!* Millie was struck twice; but she has a short fuse, my Millie, and when she's in a rage she lashes out. She grabbed the fat one—the er, widow

The Hidey-Hole

Sparleyfart—by the hair, then: *Wham! Wham! Wham!*—the blows rained down like hailstones! Me, I'd have left the women, to sort themselves out, we men to do likewise—I mean there's no sense in mixing it—but, unprovoked your honour, and I emphasise that, the wee sparleyfart springs up like the devil incarnate and flings himself on the top of my wife—'Ah, but no no! Ah, but no, my friend, we'll have less of that,' says I, introducing him to the knuckle end of my fist, the cheeky cock sparrow—and *Boom! Boom!* One to the nose, and one in the slats; and that was all there was to it! Well, he flung up his arms and he flung out his legs, and he landed—flat on his back, clean into the water, and slap-bang in the middle of my placid pool, the pearl of my precious hidey-hole. I would have fished him out straight away your worship, if I'd had time to think; but for good measure, the fat one had got the upper hand over my Millie, and was giving her what for!

"I see now that I should not have gone to my dear wife's assistance while the poor man was shipping water, but I had no idea in the heat of the moment that he was going to drown—says I to myself, 'It'll cool him off'—so I hastened away to separate the ladies; and in so doing, sustained punches, scratches and bites—Lord above, what teeth! All in all, it must have taken me five minutes, maybe ten, to prise apart those two viragoes. Well, in the end I turned round. Nothing. The water as calm as a millpond; those on the opposite bank yelling 'Fish him out! Fish him out!' That's all well and good, your lordship, but I can't swim; and foolishly diving in would only have made matters worse.

"At last the lock-keeper arrived, and two men with gaffs; that must have taken a good quarter of an hour. He was found at the very bottom of the pool that is the pride and joy of my hidey-hole, under eight feet of water, as I hereby testify; and there he was, the poor wee sparleyfart, to whom as God is my judge, I never wished a ha'p'orth of harm. Those are the bare facts, to which I swear; I am innocent of any crime, your lordship, upon my honour."

The witnesses having corroborated his evidence, and the ladies' testimonies being inadmissable because of their affray, the defendant was acquitted, and the case dismissed.

Strolling Players

Home And Away

This is an original tale. It is, to an extent, autobiographical, making due allowance, of course, for the customary licence and hoped-for hyperbole of the fireside yarn-spinner. That said, the succession of events, or something very similar, actually took place during a Field Day tour of Brian Friel's adaptation of The Three Sisters, *and my travelling companions were the actors Patrick Waldron and the late Michael Duffy.*

I hope that the amateur players of Tuam, County Galway may remember our passage through their town with some amusement, though that little episode is merely a prelude to the real story, which unfolded the following morning on O'Brien's Bridge in Galway City. The anonymous gentleman-of-the-road that I encountered that day is its hero, and our discourse, though keenly observed by some stout fellows across the road who were obviously out of earshot, was otherwise unwitnessed.

Later, in Eyre Square, I came upon a jewel of a man with arched brows, hooded eyelids and slightly retrousse nose, a pipe in his left hand and balancing a manuscript upon his knees. There, carved in stone, was the seated figure of Padraic O'Conaire, Galway's most celebrated storyteller; and gazing into his pensive, impassive face, I felt that I, too, had a story that was worth the telling.

Strolling Players

Strabane, Ballyshannon, Sligo, Tobercurry, Charlestown, Claremorris—we had motored west and south in the old Ford van for the entire afternoon, travelling a hundred miles and more on variable roads, but noting suddenly the excellence of surface, and the aura of sanctity around a little place called Knock. "Ah," said Michael, "these must be the approaches to Monsignor Horan's new airport; a dream that becomes more credible with every passing day."

"Good God," said I blasphemously, "in the middle of Connaught!"

"And why not?" asked Michael. "The Monsignor is a practical visionary."

Our discourse rambled on sporadically, touching on the economics and feasibility of such a project, on the phenomenon of Lourdes, and other weighty matters such as the fine seasonal weather—it was late summer, and the year was 1981 as I remember—but right now it had become decision time.

Our destination was Galway City; should we head for Ballinrobe and skirt Lough Corrib, or should we risk going through Tuam, the birthplace of our colleague in the back seat, and face the possibility of not reaching Galway that night? Patrick had mentioned the likelihood of such an outcome and begged us not to contemplate it, but right now he was sound asleep and snoring, and for this reason took no part in our discussion. Meanwhile, Michael had missed the turning and gone down the colourful main thoroughfare of Claremorris, remarking gleefully, "We'll resurrect our man slap bang in the middle of his native town, outside a likely-looking hostelry of course; sure you'd never hazard a guess what might ensue!"

Wouldn't you know! Parking up, and poking our heads round the door of a fine looking establishment, we enquired if anyone was acquainted with our friend, who was, I may add, still sound asleep in the back of the van. At the mere mention of this fact, the entire pub emptied out into the street to inspect him, for as luck would have it, the local dramatic society had foregathered there to discuss their next project. Imagine the look of disbelief on Pat's face on seeing former colleagues peering in at every window. Your man was something of a local hero, being the only professional performer from a town of gifted amateurs, and jealousy being entirely alien there, he, along with Michael and myself, were right royally fêted by the part-time thespians. Our company was touring *The Three Sisters* though unhappily we had none of the actresses with us in the van, which was a disappointment to one and all; but Chekov and his works were a natural topic of conversation. I was astonished at the erudition of one venerable old performer who could quote verbatim from the plays, and descant on their author's idiosyncrasies, or his dialogues and debates with Stanislavsky. Then, unexpectedly, he took me to one side and whispered darkly in my ear: "Just one word of advice. Don't be coming out with any cracks about the closure of the sugar factory; it wouldn't go down at all well!" Apparently the Irish government's refusal to bail out the sugar industry in Tuam was a very sore point with the locals; but I have to say, I have racked my brains ever since as to how this very knowledgeable old boy could possibly have envisaged Colonel Vershinin stepping out of character in order to deliver a jibe at the expense of the good folk of Tuam. I thanked him warmly at the time, however, and some hour or so afterwards, Michael drove us safely and sedately into Galway city.

The following morning, I was taking the air to clear my head when I observed, just to one side of a picturesque bridge, O'Brien's I believe, a fair-sized group of men of the itinerant inclination. A second glance confirmed that they were full members of the fortified wine-bibbing fraternity and no doubt part-time moonshiners—harmless enough in their way, but somehow disturbing at that time of the morning, in such large numbers—and myself with none too clear a head. Not wishing to seem to be giving them a wide berth, I crossed the road, but walked towards, then past them, pausing in the centre of the bridge, where, leaning on the parapet, I gazed steadfastly into the slow-flowing stream.

Presently, I became aware of a powerful aroma—an all-pervading aerial cocktail of cheap biddy, strong cider, and possibly rough, raw poteen. I knew at once that I had company; a pair of elbows other than my own, rested on the parapet beside me. I turned and saw a dark, livid countenance, not unhandsome but deeply lined and weathered by years of exposure to strong drink and the elements. For all that, he was still striking in appearance and had a fine head of blue black hair, albeit thickly matted and in need of a trim and a wash. At first, the only sound was a strangled wheeze as air was expelled from clogged up lungs and a half-blocked windpipe. Then a gentle Galway brogue murmured softly, "That's a brave looking sort of day now."

"It is," said I, "and looks set to stay that way."

"You're a stranger I'd say," said the man affably. "You sound to me like a man from the North Country."

"Oh aye," says I, "from the north of Ireland."

"Oh now," says he with a wink, "I've heard tell some folk up there think that's debatable ..." and he roared with laughter at his own quick wit and perspicacity, making himself cough and splutter into the bargain.

"I tell you what it is," he said in a hoarse whisper. "You'll have noticed the crowd of us hanging about at the corner—there's not usually that many of us in the one spot; but the truth is we've been through a bit of an ordeal. They put us on the television last night and made a bit of a spectacle out of us; well, they had to, really. They were attempting to draw attention to our plight, especially in the winter months, and some woman from Dublin was campaigning to get some sort of a roof over our heads, a shelter of some kind, for the bitter cold nights from December to February. I suppose it was for effect, but they turned hoses on us to give the impression of rain and make us look more pathetic; it was a fairly humiliating experience I may tell you; but sure, eventually, some good may come of it. Oh, fair play! They gave us soup and sandwiches, and even a drink or two, but now they've all packed up and gone, and we're more down in the dumps and no better off than we were before; and for good measure didn't we all get soaked to the skin; drenched and frozen to the marrow! I feel partly to blame for I talked some of them into it—to tell you the truth, mister, they've asked me to get a few bob together ..." he trailed off lamely, then added defiantly, "Ah, sure there's no use swinging the lead to a clear-headed man like yourself; we only want it for more drink!" I felt around awkwardly for a note in my rear pocket, and extracted one discreetly, unaware of its denomination, as your man continued his pitch.

"They've made me their spokesman you see, because I suppose I have retained something of what we call the gift of the gab. That is to say I can string a few words, even a sentence or two together to make an ounce of sense ... to put a case, or plead a cause. Some of the lads say I'd have made a good lawyer, but I don't think I'd have embraced that blaggardly profession, whatever cards life had dealt me." He broke off his discourse to eye me quizzically for a moment, then added, "I trust you are not a legal gentleman yourself, sir; but I'd say not, if I'm any judge of character." Though this last comment was not a direct question, it somehow required an answer, and the polite pause which followed gave me the opportunity to provide one—the persuasive art of the diplomat.

"Lord save us, no," says I, with some warmth, for I shared along with Charles Dickens, his robust contempt for the law, or at least for some of its well-heeled, cynical practitioners. "I have, like yourself, however," I continued lamely, "on occasion played the role of advocate; I am a stroller by profession, and we are performing here at the Jesuit Hall for just half a week."

He regarded me suddenly in a completely new

light, and stepped back a pace to assess me. "A stroller, begod! A strolling player—I'd never have guessed it— you have neither the swagger of a court fop, nor the autocratic air of a Prince of Denmark, but I'd not doubt you have the spirit for it; it takes some spunk, I'd say, to tread the boards! And whose play would you be presenting now, may I ask?"

"A play by Anton Chekov," said I, "the Russian writer."

"Oh, I've heard of him, alright—a doctor, wasn't he? And what class of a part now, would you be enacting?"

"A colonel," I replied diffidently, "Colonel Vershinin." I was about to add something foolish about Russian troops picketing the sugar factory at Tuam, but thought better of it. Meanwhile, out of the corner of my eye, I could sense that I was being shrewdly appraised by a critical, unblinking gaze. The judgement when it came was cautiously favourable: "Oh, I'd credit that alright. I'd say you'd be just the boy to play a colonel, though the northern brogue might be a handicap."

We gazed into the water for a while, then my companion continued. "The only other actor I've ever met was Mr. Anew McMaster. Did you ever come across him?"

"Oh, I had the good fortune when young to see his Hamlet and his Othello," said I, "performances which I shall never forget; but I met him only the once, backstage at the Olympia Theatre, Dublin in 1960. He was then, I believe, over eighty years of age; a great man in our profession," I added.

"A great man in any profession," said my friend, his bloodshot eyes gleaming brightly, "and a great actor. Oh yes, a very great actor indeed ..." his voice trailed off, and he gazed into the far distance as though stirred by some cherished memory etched upon the fuddled brain. I did not presume to invade his private dream ... but after what seemed an eternity, he said in a soft voice, "I was once on stage with Mr. McMaster ..." then after a pause he added, "at Oughterard, I think it was." My full attention was aroused instantly. I had no reason to disbelieve a word this man said, so I waited for the full story.

"I was only a boy at the time, and a mob of us were milling about outside the hall where the celebrated actor and his company were performing that evening. A man who they told me was a stage manager walked over and picked me out, saying he would give me a sixpence if I ran onto the stage in the middle of the performance and gave Mr. McMaster a message; it was something about a burning wood coming to Luton or Dunstable, or some place like that. After some few hours of hanging about and insistent efforts to instil the message into my unschooled memory cells, the cue to enter arrived; I was tapped on the shoulder and I ran on with my news. Well, the great man, who didn't look at all well, grabbed hold of me in a towering rage and near shook the life out of me, at the same time putting a fearful curse on me and calling me a liar. As soon as he let go of me, I ran off like a scalded cat, but not before shouting back at him that it's what I'd been told to say by that whoor of a stage manager. And do you know sir, I got a rousing cheer from the crowd for standing up for meself."

I made no comment. The tale is legendary; but had I, by some miracle, met the very man who was that boy? Or was he just indulging that time-honoured Irish custom of spinning a good yarn and passing it off as his own? Who can tell! To have queried him further would have been ungracious; and after all, truth is often stranger than fiction. Time after time we have evidence of the old saying about it being a small world. An almost golden silence ensued of the kind that has the aura of the eternal about it, a sense of time suspended—what Camus has described as a feeling of arrival, of the heart standing still. The silence was broken eventually, but not the mood; the river mirrored an azure sky, and the sky was infinite space.

"As you have no doubt twigged," said the man from Oughterard or thereabouts, "I'm a bit of a stroller myself; that's the rest of the troupe across the street— but we're only a loose alliance, a thing of threads and patches. 'How did this all come to pass?' you may be wondering; I'm not taking up too much of your time am I?" said he.

"Not at all," said I.

He whistled a snatch from 'The Galway Shawl' as he marshalled his thoughts, and I in turn, mutely recalled these words:

"She wore no jewels, no costly diamonds

No paint or powder, no none at all ..."

After an intake of breath, he began his tale:

"I was just a young fellow like many another, full of life and spirit, and in love with the best-looking girl to be seen for many a mile; though it wasn't just her looks I may tell you. I like to think we were kindred spirits; indeed, two halves of but one single soul. She was all I'd ever wanted in a woman, and all I'd want still, God help me. I had fond parents, but I was the youngest of six brothers and the farm was small, so wanting only the best for the girl of my dreams, I had this notion to cross the water and seek my fortune. Fortune, indeed! I made a bob or two all right carryin' hods and diggin' up roads, but it all seemed to go by the end of the week. Maybe my fellow exiles and myself had a constitutional weakness for conviviality, coupled with a yearning for home and a need to drown that yearning. Whatever the reasons, there was, after several years, no hint of the nest egg I had envisaged. I scribbled fond notes from time to time, but I was never a scholar and expressing my feelings on paper never came easy. In desperation, I embarked, almost penniless, on a boat for America; there, surely, my fortunes would take a turn for the better. It was not to be. My mental state was low, and I longed for home and the girl I'd left behind. Several more years elapsed before I could scrape together the fare home, but by now I had given up writing, and I was too proud to admit failure. A twelvemonth later I crawled back to my native place.

"My eldest brother was running the farm and would barely speak to me. The other brothers and my parents had died while I was in the States; and the love of my life was wed to another and living in England. The next oldest brother to me, and the closest, was away at sea; in fact I had bumped into him at Southampton once, oh, years before. I drank what money I had left on me in the local pub, then walked away from it all; and I have been walking ever since.

"Well, there you have it, Mister—my full and frank confession, which I am not in the habit of recounting to new acquaintances; I hope you'll take that as a compliment."

"Indeed I do," said I.

"You're a good listener, for an actor," said he with a wry smile. "By the way," he continued, "I never lusted after, nor have I lifted a leg over another woman; my own dear sweetheart, God bless her, was my one and only love ... now the last person I said that to was a priest, and that was a long time ago—her only rival I suppose, was the little brown jug."

He gave me a perfunctory salute and began to walk

away. "Wait," I said, "Surely the men are expecting ..."

"Ah, me bollocks," he replied, "They'd only be drinking whatever you gave us and be roarin' by midday, myself not excepted. Sure you are only a poor stroller like ourselves, and the work is hard to come by in your trade, they tell me; and forbye all that, the Jesuit hall in Galway is hardly Broadway. Good luck to you anyway and welcome to Connemara; and may the road rise with you my friend, and the sun be always at your back."

I must still have looked uneasy, for he was quick to re-assure me—"Don't worry your head now, mister honey, sure in holy Ireland another benefactor may be just around the corner; we have kind hearts most of us, thanks be to God! I'll give your regards to the Jesuits and they'll surely give us our dinner."

"Come on, men," he roared, waving his troupe into line and heading straight for the Jesuit establishment down the road. A born leader, I thought—an intuitive general at the head of a harmless little army; and not a bad bone in his body—oh that Ireland, north, south, east, and west, had more leaders of his calibre, his integrity, and his goodwill.

The ten-pound note remained folded in the palm

of my hand, but the moment had passed. To have called him back and created a spectacle, would only have dented his pride. Later that day, I placed it in the Jesuit's mission box; I only hope his army got their dinner.

Scully's Goat

❖

Home And Away

At the request of worried parents, I wrote to young Gogarty the other day—no connection with the illustrious Oliver St. John—just an aspiring young poet starving in a London garret, believing against all the odds that somewhere in this literary mecca there were cobblestones of gold.

"Dear Declan," I began—for that is his name—"A little bird tells me that you have turned down a plum job with the Irish Times, *as a reviewer of plays, no less! Think again, dear boy, think again!" At a loss for words to pursue my doubtless unwelcome advice, I suddenly recalled a charming story by Alphonse Daudet, prefaced by an imaginary letter to 'Monsieur Pierre Gringoire, Lyric Poet, at Paris'. Gringoire, born in Normandy in the latter part of the fifteenth century, appears in Hugo's* Nôtre Dame de Paris, *and in the novel marries Esmeralda, the beautiful young woman who is always accompanied by her pet goat. Unashamedly, I decided to paraphrase Daudet's letter to Gringoire, and retell his story in my own words, purely for young Declan's benefit you understand. Hence—*

Scully's Goat

You will never change, my poor lad! Who do you think you are, to turn down such an offer! I mean, look at yourself, you unfortunate boy—down at heel shoes, threadbare suit, gaunt features crying out for a square meal—this is what comes of your passion for poetry, this is your reward for ten years loyal service to Lord Apollo; have you no shame at the end of all! Become a critic, you fool! Become a critic! You will earn some precious gold sovereigns, you will have a reserved table at your favourite Dublin restaurant, and you will attend first nights with a brand new pen tucked into your breast pocket ... No? You don't wish to? You value your freedom, and will continue to do so to the bitter end? All well and good, my boy ... but pin your lugs back, and hear the cautionary tale of Scully's Goat; learn what's to be gained by the wish to live at liberty.

***

Scully never had much luck with his goats. He lost them all in the selfsame way. One fine morning they'd break loose from their tether, take themselves off up the mountain, and once there, they'd be eaten by the big bad wolf—that was the story anyhow—not their master's loving care, not fear of the wolf, nothing held them back. These were, it would appear, independent-minded goats, valuing above all else, freedom, fresh air, and wide open spaces.

The bould Scully, decent cratur' that he was, who understood nothing of the character of his beasts, came to the conclusion that himself and goats just didn't hit it off together.

"That's it," said he, "Goats fret when they're with me. I'll have to give them up!"

Yet despite this, he persisted, and after losing six goats in the same way, he bought a seventh; only this time he took the precaution of acquiring her very young, so that in time she might become inured to staying with him.

Ah, Declan, how pretty she was, this little goat of Mr. Scully, so very, very pretty with her soft eyes, her little tufted 'goatee' beard, her glossy black hooves, her striped horns; and her long white fleece like a charming little loose-fitting overcoat! Almost the equal of Esmeralda's adorable little kid in the opera— surely you've seen the pictures, Declan—and then, docile, loving, allowing herself to be milked without fretting, and never putting her foot in the pail; a wee dote of a goat.

Mr. Scully had a paddock hedged in by hawthorn at the back of his residence. It was here he placed his new lodger, attaching her to a post at the most beautiful spot in the meadow, taking care to give her plenty of rope; and every so often he would come and visit, to make sure she was all right. The goat seemed very happy, and cropped the grass with such good will that Mr. Scully was delighted—at last, thought the poor man, here is a goat that doesn't pine to be with me.

Poor Scully was mistaken. His goat was pining. One day she said to herself, gazing up at the mountain, "How good it must be up there! What bliss to gambol among the heather without the hindrance of this accursed rope which chafes my neck. It's one thing for the ox or the ass to graze in a field—goats need their freedom!"

From that moment, the grass of the meadow

seemed to her insipid. Boredom set in. She grew thin, her milk came rarely. It was pitiful to see her tug all day at her rope, her head toward the mountain side, her nostrils flaring, and crying 'Ma-aa', oh, so dolefully.

Mr. Scully soon noticed that something was amiss with his goat, but knew not what it was ... one morning whilst trying to milk her, she turned to him and spoke in her own dialect—

"Dear Mr. Scully, I am languishing here. Let me go to the mountain."

"Ah, dear God, she also?" cried Mr. Scully in stupefaction, and he let the pail fall from his grasp. Then sitting on the ground beside his goat, he sighed in disbelief.

"Oh, Snowdrop! You wish to leave me?"

And Snowdrop replied, "Yes, Mr. Scully."

"Is it the grass that's not to your liking?"

"Oh no, Mr. Scully."

"Perhaps you are on too short a leash. Shall I lengthen the rope?"

"That is not the problem, Mr. Scully."

"Then what must I do for you, what is your wish?"

"I wish to go to the mountain, Mr. Scully."

"But, poor creature, know you not that there is a wolf on the mountain; what will you do when he comes?"

"I will butt him with my horns, Mr. Scully."

"The wolf will sneer at your horns. He has eaten old nanny goats more endowed with horns than yourself. Surely you remember old Martha who was here last year—a tough old boot as strong and fierce as any buck—she did battle with the wolf all night long! Then at dawn, the wolf devoured her."

"Bless me! Poor Martha! But it makes no difference, Mr. Scully. Please let me go to the mountain."

"Goodness gracious," said Mr. Scully, "What has become of my goats! All but one, the wolf has swallowed! But no, I will save you in spite of yourself, you little hussy; and for fear you should break your rope, I will lock you up in the byre, there to remain always."

There and then, Scully carried off the goat to a darkened cowshed, and locked the door with a double bolt. Unfortunately, he forgot about the window, and scarcely had he turned his back when the little rascal was up, off, and away.

"You laugh, Declan. By Jove, I believe you take the part of the goat against poor Mr. Scully; in time, you may laugh on the other side of your face".

When the pretty white goat arrived on the mountain, enchantment reigned all around. Never had the old Scots pines set eyes on a thing so lovely. She was received like a little queen. The chestnut trees bowed low to the earth to caress her with the tops of their branches. The golden gorse parted to make way for her, and gave out scent for all it was worth. The entire mountain paid her homage.

Just think, Declan, how happy our goat was! No more rope, no more stake, nothing to impede her frolicking, or grazing at will. Right there was the grass, dear fellow, just beneath her horns, and what grass! Juicy, fine, serrated, seasoned with a thousand herbs— quite another thing to the turf of her paddock—and then the flowers! Great bluebells, purple foxgloves— an entire forest of wild flora exuding heady nectar!

The white goat, half-drunk, simply wallowed in it, legs in the air; and rolled along mossy banks, pell-mell with the falling chestnut leaves, before all at once, landing upright on her feet with a single bound— hup! Watch her set off head first through thorn and thicket, one moment on a precipice, another in a ravine, windswept crag, or silent valley—high, low, everywhere—one might have thought that Scully had ten goats on the mountain! She feared nothing, did Snowdrop.

She'd emerge with a leap from mighty torrents which drenched her with moisture and milk-white spray, then dripping wet she'd recline stretched out on some smooth rock, there to dry herself in the sun. One time, venturing onto a dizzy ledge, a laburnum bloom clenched in her teeth, she saw, far below, Mr. Scully's house with its paddock at the rear; it made her laugh until she cried.

"How small it is," said she. How could I bear to stay there, so cooped up?"

Poor Snowdrop! To see herself so perched on high, she believed she was as big as the whole wide world.

All in all, this was a red letter day for Scully's little goat. Around midday, scampering to right and left, she fell in with a herd of deer in the act of stripping a wild vine with bared teeth. Our little vagabond in the fluffy white overcoat was a sensation! She was given pride of place at the feast, and all the stags were very gentlemanly and on their best behaviour. It would even appear—and this is strictly confidential, young man—that a young buck with a coal-black coat had the good fortune to take Snowdrop's fancy. The pair of sweethearts wandered through the woods together for an hour or two, and if you want to know what passed between them, go and consult those babbling brooks which flow unseen among the moss.

Suddenly, the wind freshened. The mountain turned purple; it was evening.

"Already!" said the little goat, as she stood stock-still, quite astonished.

Down below, the fields were shrouded in mist. Mr. Scully's paddock disappeared from sight, and of the little house, only the roof, and a faint trail of smoke could be seen. She heard the tinkling bells of a flock returning home and felt a wistful sadness come over her. A hawk, wheeling homeward, brushed her with his wings as he passed by. She shuddered fearfully. A prolonged howl echoed across the mountainside, "Hou! Hou!" She at once thought of the wolf—all day long the foolish creature had not given it a thought—at the same moment, a horn sounded far down in the valley; it was the good Mr. Scully trying one last effort.

"Hou! Hou!" howled the wolf.

"Come home! Come home!" cried the horn.

Snowdrop felt an urge to return, but recalling the stake, the rope, the hawthorn hedge around the paddock, she felt she could no longer submit to that life, and it was better to remain where she was. The horn ceased to sound.

The goat heard behind her a rustling of leaves, and turning round she saw in the shadows two short ears, bolt upright, with two eyes which gleamed in the dark. It was the wolf.

Enormous, motionless, seated upon its hindquarters, it was there, surveying the little white goat and savouring it in advance. Since he knew for sure he was going to eat her, he was in no hurry; only when she turned round he began to laugh wickedly, "Ho! Ho! Ho! Mr. Scully's little goat!" he leered, and passed his great red tongue across his burning chops.

Snowdrop felt herself utterly lost—one moment, in recalling the story of old Martha who fought all night long only to be eaten in the morning, she said to herself that perhaps it would be better to be devoured straight away; then, changing her mind, she prepared to defend herself, head lowered, horns presented, like

the brave little goat that she was—not that she held
out any hope of killing her adversary; goats do not kill
the wolf—but simply to see if she could hold out
longer than Martha.

Now the beast advanced, and the little horns began
to dance.

Ah, brave little goat! How she set about her task
with a stout heart! More than ten times—I tell no lie
Declan—she made the wolf retreat to reconsider and
catch its breath. During these breaks of around a
minute's duration, the little gourmand gathered in
haste a bunch of her favourite grass, then returned to
the fray with mouth full—this procedure lasted all
night long. From time to time Scully's little goat
looked up at the stars dancing in a cloudless sky, and
said to herself, "Oh, that I may last out till daybreak!"

One after another the stars went out. Snowdrop
redoubled the blows from her horns as the wolf
stepped up the gnashing of murderous teeth. A pale
glow appeared on the horizon. The hoarse crowing of
a cock rose up from a farmyard far below.

"At last!" cried the poor little creature, who had
wished for nothing more than daybreak in order to
die; and she stretched herself full-length upon the

ground, her lovely white fleece all stained and spattered with blood. Then the wolf threw himself on the little white goat, and ate her.

***

That's all for now, Declan. The story you have just heard is not a tale of my invention. If you're down in 'Tyrone Among the Bushes', somewhere near the foot of the Sperrin Mountains—say below Bessy Bell or Ballynatubbrit—the farmers there will often speak of it ... well, maybe not these days ... but bear you in mind Scully's wee goat, Master Declan, who wrought hard the whole night through in defence of her free spirit; then, come morning, the wolf ate her. Are you listening carefully, Declan, "Then come morning, the wolf ate her!"

The Pepper Pot

Home And Away

You can almost smell a story, can you not?

Like the frozen words of Francois Rabelais thawing in concert with inarticulate moans and groans on balmy days, or the half-lilt of light-headed laughter released from its ice-bound prison, it is a presence in the atmosphere, a mood, a raw sensation. Narrative comes later, as individual elements conspire to form a phrase, a sentence, a paragraph or two; but first and foremost comes the word. The word is the beginning and the beginning is the word; but grant it no supremacy, attribute not our origins to its power or its antiquity; it is a key to expression, nothing less and nothing more.

So what sets it free, this initiatory word, what causes it to melt and mingle with its airy companions and impinge upon our consciousness? Is it memory, association, a flash of lucidity? Is it being in, or conjuring up, a particular place or time? Or is it merely the warmer weather? ...

The Pepper Pot

As the ferry swung out of Loch Ryan leaving a graceful arc of turbulent white water in its wake, I got a glimpse astern of the great rock of Ailsa, known prosaicly to my father's generation as 'Paddy's Milestone'. Whilst cherishing that affectionate childhood image, I also called to mind the sonnets of the poets Keats and Wordsworth addressed to that "craggy ocean pyramid", and remembered that Keats had made the crossing from Portpatrick to Donaghadee before walking the entire southern shore of Belfast Lough, to reach the Athens of the North. Passing Portpatrick itself, as the ship hugged the rocky coastline of the Rhinns of Galloway, another vision sprang unannounced into my mind: the actress Sarah Siddons standing on the jetty declaiming lines from *Dido* to the unfeeling winds and waves—"words, words, words"—

"Methinks I stand upon some rugged beach

Sighing to winds and to the waves complaining
While afar off the vessel sails away ... "

"Egad, m'dear," remarked her less imaginative
husband, "if we don't hurry, the vessel will be gone,
absolutely."

It is hard, somehow, to envisage Keats at Castle
Junction or to conjure up Gainsborough's elegant lady
striding the boards of Belfast's old Theatre Royal, so
those tales remain, shall we say, on ice. Not so the
disaster that befell the ill-fated ferry Princess Victoria,
as we pass over the spot where she foundered and sank
so close to land. It is still too easy to evoke the howling
winds and raging billows of that dreadful storm and
the helpless, hopeless cries of drowning men and
women. "What words did they utter?" I ask myself,
and what did He who is The Word have to say by way
of comfort? The Titanic Memorial portrays victims
clutching the robes of a guardian angel; but all that is
history—

"Eternal Father, strong to save"—and so on.

My travelling companion on this journey was
Mack, an old friend, and we had touched on these
and other topics on the earlier part of the crossing.

The Pepper Pot

Like myself, Mack was a half-exiled Ulsterman who
had resided for the last twenty-five years or so in and
around Dumfries, first as the hospitable landlord of a
tavern in that fine town, later working on the
construction of the bypass, and then in the local
telephone exchange where, as operator, he picked up
the first distress calls of the Lockerbie air disaster
which he recalled as "cries from the inferno". The
most active part of his life had been spent in the RAF,
first as a fighter pilot and latterly in helicopters as part
of the search and rescue service. Before that, he had
served his time as a plumber, working for a man he
affectionately called 'Old Johnny Campbell', though I
imagined that by now Johnny was not so much old, as
deceased. The work was often on attachment to, or
subcontracted from, Harland & Wolff's shipyard. A
man of parts, his varied life and career meant he was
full of tales of adventure, humour, and indeed tragedy,
though he seldom dwelt on the latter. Many years ago
he had been put in charge of enquiries into the death
of a fellow fighter pilot who had taken off from
Dishforth in Yorkshire and crashed into the mud and
silt of the River Ouse at Selby; the young widow was
obviously in great distress and Mack did what he

could to comfort her. Time went by and they met again by chance, fell in love, and were married, having a long and happy life together; but only recently, Mack had lost his beloved Irene, and this was his first trip home since her death.

As the boat nosed its way up the Lough, and his keen eyes scanned the County Down coastline, fond memories and nostalgic recollections were self-evident but largely unexpressed; though his first airborne exploits with the Newtownards flying club were, I am sure, among them. It was just as we entered the mouth of the river that his face really lit up, however, and his eyes took on an added sparkle: "Puh! Puh! Puh!" he almost stammered as we drew level with a mooring at the Deep Water Wharf, then, taking a deep breath, snapping his fingers and pointing to an exact spot, he gave utterance and spat it out. "*The Pepper Pot*," he exclaimed. "That's where she was fitted out and refurbished." The word, or words had thawed; a story had begun.

Cranes and gantries loomed overhead, and a characterless container ship occupied the berth Mack had indicated but the low hills of Castlereagh and Craigantlet still formed a timeless backdrop, and between them and the reclaimed land of Sydenham—by the muddy banks of Connswater, in the Shangri La of Victoria Park—stretched all my childhood days; what memories flooded back as we leaned over the ship's rail.

"Yes," said Mack, "she had been a luxury liner, but *The Pepper Pot* was what we called her, because she was so full of holes from her wartime battering—more holes than hull in fact—oh, she was a fighter, this proud vessel, and survived the entire hostilities of World War II.

"So what was her name then?" I enquired, "This wreck of an ocean liner unrecognisable from her pre-war glory days?"

"*The Queen of the Pacific*," Mack murmured softly.

The name rang distant bells from my teens when my sheet-metal worker father worked in the shipyard. Was there not some tragedy attached to her war service? I would look up her story later but meanwhile, a sleek, gleaming white hull, a streamlined superstructure and two buff-coloured funnels sailed into my mind's eye as Mack hinted at some calamity connected to her sea trials; though the story uppermost in his mind was a much more personal and intimate one, as a wry smile playing about his lips and a narrowing of the eyes indicated ... but, to begin at the beginning, to begin, with the word—

The *Reina del Pacifico*, which of course means the 'Queen of the Pacific' was built at Harland & Wolff's for the Pacific Steam Navigation Company. Her ship's number was 852, her tonnage 17,100 and she was the first passenger ship of that line whose name did not begin with an O. Her launch date was 23rd September 1930, her delivery date was for March of the following year, and her maiden voyage from Liverpool to Valparaiso began on 9th April 1931.

She was powered by four twelve-cylinder blast-injection, trunk-piston diesel engines; of her two beige funnels, the fore was a dummy. Her hull was indeed gleaming white, with her waterline a bright emerald green; as handsome a luxury ship as any afloat at the time. It was on board the *Reina del Pacifico* that the first British Labour Prime Minister, Mr. Ramsay MacDonald, died in November 1937, bound for a holiday in South America. His body was put ashore in Bermuda and lay in state in Nassau Cathedral. Commandeered as a troop ship on the outbreak of war, the vessel had many wartime adventures—in the North Atlantic off Narvik, in the Mediterranean off the North African coast and participating in the Sicily landings; twice to Bombay and back via Cape Town—she was attacked many times both at sea and in port, and though repeatedly damaged, was rarely out of commission. She carried countless service personnel, and sailed some 350,000 miles, the equivalent of fourteen times around the globe. Another highlight was the safe conduct of the King and Queen of Yugoslavia into exile, a mission accomplished without incident.

Decommissioned at Liverpool, she was in the Canada graving dock for a spell where she was the subject of some security scares in March 1946, a naked flame being found unattended in her hold. Soon afterwards she arrived in Belfast for a thorough refit, the job to be accomplished in time for her first post-war sailing to take place in October of the same year. Work on that refit was nearing a conclusion when, in late summer, Mack entered the story: "You will have three weeks," Johnny Campbell told him, "to install a deluxe, and I mean deluxe bathroom suite in the principal first-class stateroom. The bath itself, a sunken affair, is enormous; and the entire set—bath, shower, bidet, wash-basins and separate toilets—is in shining black enamel with goldleaf trim, gold-framed mirrors and gleaming gold taps. The bath itself is far too big to get in by the normal door, so the entire bulkhead, facings and all, will be removed until the suite is installed, and then replaced; that, of course, will involve practically every trade in the book." And so it was that Mack set to his task—"the whole jing-bang has cost a fortune," Johnny had added, "so handle all components with kid gloves and the utmost care!"

Welders, riveters, boilermakers, platers, sheet-metal workers, fitters, electricians, shipwrights, joiners, painters, plasterers—you name it—all had assisted at the cautious dismantling of the bulkhead and witnessed the arrival of the sybaritic toilet suite, everything laid on cushioned surfaces, everything supervised as for a state visit. Managerial hawks with colourful nicknames like 'Air Raid', and 'The Brown Bomber' were in close attendance, fussing and cooing like ladies-in-waiting around a royal cradle, the great sunken receptacle itself was of course the focus of attention, the object of every gloating eye. Imagine the collective envy of men whose humble zinc contraption hung from a rusty nail on the backyard door, to be hauled in front of the fire on a Friday night and filled from kettles and saucepans heated over a kitchen range—if his luck was in his missus might scrub his back—what would he give to wallow in this opulent tub, with turbaned odalisques trailing languid limbs in scented water, and semi-naked slave girls swathed in sumptuous towels on hand with aromatic oils and oleaginous unguents. Only that latter day Pharaoh, King Farouk of Egypt—he with the roving eye and the Midas touch—could match such a fabulous bathtub, or so it was rumoured.

But, interest died down as is inevitable; though within the fortnight, when everything was more or less in place and the trades returned to hoist the bulkhead back into position, securing it once and for all to the outer hull, curiosity fleetingly returned. The overall effect was indeed one of unbridled opulence and luxury, and the horney-handed men of manual toil gawped goggle-eyed and begrudgingly: "Some lucky bastards have it all ways," they concluded with one accord, mutely expressing a post-war *ennui* endorsed by disillusioned servicemen returning to

Civvy Street. It was almost a relief when the barrier was raised and daylight, along with an understandable resentment, was blotted out.

Outside, on the bulkhead's exposed face, the various trades drilled, hammered, welded and riveted; sawed, planed, buffed and painted—each trade careful not to overstep its mark or infringe another's rights, for this was the heyday of demarcation, when one man stood aside to await another's pleasure— riveters could drill holes up to a quarter inch diameter and no more; above that! a boilermaker was required, if one could be found—but one example of many strictly drawn lines! Inside, drowned out by all the clamour, Mack beavered away quietly, the men outside scarcely aware of his existence; an odd fitter tinkering or a fleeting painter touching up might pass through the narrow door from time to time, but virtually everything—fittings and furnishings, tiles, mirrors, concealed lights, floor coverings, bath mats, heated towel rails—all were in place; and as Mack gave a last half-turn to a recalcitrant gold nut, and flicked away a final speck of dust, the job was complete. It was Thursday mid-afternoon and the task had been accomplished a day ahead of schedule.

The Pepper Pot

The young plumber, aglow with job satisfaction and justifiable pride, closed the narrow door behind him and reported back to his boss.

"Good work, Mack," said old Johnny, "we'll have her inspected on Monday morning and that will be that. It should take place around eleven o'clock I'd say; no doubt upper management will want to poke their noses in—it's such a showpiece!"

On Monday morning, at eleven o'clock on the dot, Johnny and Mack awaited the arrival of the inspection party. The door was self-locking so one of their number would have the necessary keys. About five minutes past, a group of officials duly arrived, and an impressive looking bunch they were: two brown overalls, two hard hats, the official inspector, the head draughtsman, the deputy managing director no less, and a couple of other VIP's arrived, all smiles and brimming with anticipation. The party of nine squeezed through the narrow entrance, traversed the ornately panelled apartment and stepped inside the spacious toilet suite; Johnny Campbell and Mack brought up the rear. What greeted them was a collective expression of consternation and disbelief written all over their dumbstruck features. Mack

followed their astonished gaze and looked towards the
pièce de résistance—it had gone, vanished, disappeared
without trace; and the gleaming golden taps hung
impotently over a gaping hole. Words are not up to
the task of describing the scene—deflation, anti-
climax and suppressed anger perhaps covers the
general mood, but one sensed also the ghastly finger
of suspicion as all eyes turned a cold gaze of disbelief
on the equally bewildered Mack. Very soon he found
himself isolated as the group huddled round Johnny
Campbell demanding some sort of explanation.
Finally, the party decamped and moved in a body
elsewhere leaving Mack as a solitary witness of the
scene of desolation. A hard hat, in fact, ordered Mack
to stay where he was, but Johnny overruled him and
told his plumber to report for work the following
morning. In the event, he wandered off to a quiet
dockside pub and sat for hours trying to find a
solution to an insoluble puzzle. What magic power
could transpose or translocate such a massive artefact,
cast, what is more, in one piece, through a solid steel
bulkhead when the only aperture was a narrow door
many times too small to accommodate it?

There was no answer to this mighty conundrum of

course, and a series of low-key, inconclusive enquiries plainly bore this out. Johnny went through the activities of his plumber from the last turn of the spanner and the closing of the door, right through to his reappearance on the scene of inspection; they checked out together whether any dubious characters had made any enquiries about the bath or its value. The management surreptitiously questioned anyone who might have had access to it over the weekend; theft was the obvious and indeed only explanation, but the hard facts indicated that its removal was impossible other than by some supernatural or paranormal agency. Further detective work became positively embarrassing, and the firm opted for hushing things up and getting on with a replacement, at considerable expense of course. Neither Johnny Campbell's firm or Mack were involved in this operation of course, and both Johnny and Mack in particular remained under a bit of a cloud. Eventually the whole thing was forgotten and fizzled out, and meanwhile the entire refit of the *Reina de Pacifico* was completed.

There was an aftermath, or sequel to the tale—two in fact. The first concerned that 'tragic aura'

unconnected with her war service. The explanation
for this was, alas, all too imminent. On the night of
Thursday 11th September 1947, the ship was
returning from speed trials conducted in the Firth of
Clyde, satisfactory except for slight overheating in one
of the engines, all four of which had been installed
when the vessel was built in 1931. On the homeward
journey, approaching the entrance to the Lough and
while speed was being increased, all four engines blew
up without warning reducing the engine room to a
shambles and causing extensive damage to other parts
of the great liner, especially amidships. An eyewitness
who went out in a tender to help the injured said,
"You would not know the ship. She is badly bashed
up. The bulkheads are twisted and her decks are up."
An enquiry concluded that over-heating in one of the
cylinders had ignited gases in the crankshaft of one
engine causing an explosion which had detonated the
other three. In all, 28 people died and a further 23
were injured. The only medical man on board at the
time of the disaster was a Dr. Hamilton of Bangor
who was still in his twenties. He toiled heroically for
three hours wading knee-deep in oil and debris, and
freeing those who were trapped; he personally

attended to and bandaged nearly sixty cases before further assistance arrived. The injured were hauled up into the first-class staterooms and no doubt that bathroom was a casualty station.

So, what of that original bath? Was the mystery ever solved? By now, my travelling companion and I had rolled off the ferry and were motoring down to Bangor. Mack's eyes narrowed.

"Well, many years after these sad events, Irene and I were celebrating an anniversary in Daly's Steak House in Dublin, a place where you could get an excellent meal and also enjoy a pint of porter without feeling or looking out of place; a convivial sort of establishment where you could settle in and get your feet under the table, so to speak. I had demolished an excellent sirloin and Irene had enjoyed a grilled Dover Sole, when a bunch of familiar looking faces burst into the place—about a dozen old shipyard colleagues on a day trip to the fair city—needless to say, greetings were exchanged, my young wife introduced and the drinks began to flow. Inevitably, the subject of the bath cropped up, and laughter rang around the room, mainly at my expense. When it died away, a man whose face I didn't recognise said softly, 'I know the answer to that one.' We were all agog! 'Yes,' he said, 'I was an outside electrician and the light-fitting above the bath was faulty. I had just slipped through the open door and was putting my gear in a corner when I heard it close; you apparently left without noticing me. I was a clumsy young beggar in those days, and used a heavy hammer to tap the old fitting loose. It slipped from my grasp and crashed onto the side of the bath chipping it badly then ricocheted on to the other side causing more damage. I was petrified. This priceless tub was ruined, and if I owned up, or questions were asked, I was for the sack, no doubt about that! What was I to do?

"'I thought for a moment before going across to the narrow teak door and shooting a couple of inside bolts. I listened to the incessant din outside and thought to myself that a bit more noise would hardly be noticed, so I picked up the heavy hammer and set to work. it took a couple of hours to reduce the big bath to fragments small enough to drop through a convenient porthole on the side of the ship away from the quay. One by one I slipped them through and as far as I know they are lying at the bottom of the deep water wharf to this day.'

"I looked him straight in the eye; if he had told me at the time what he was telling me now, I think I'd have taken him apart, but the company was congenial and it had all happened a long time ago. I suppose, in his way, he had got a guilty secret off his chest; and as for me, well it's a relief to get to the bottom of an unsolved and apparently unsolvable mystery."

Fear

Home And Away

It seemed fitting to follow a shipyard tale with a yarn told on shipboard, but although the central character exhibits some of the qualities of sang-froid and derring-do that typify a certain kind of Ulsterman, it did not seem necessary to labour the point.

Fear

We went up on the bridge again after dinner. Before us the Mediterranean, in which a big calm moon was mirrored perfectly, had not a ripple on its entire surface. The great ship moved effortlessly, throwing against the star-studded sky a huge trail of black smoke; and behind us, churned up by the propellers, and displaced by the swift passage of the heavy vessel, the wake frothed and twisted and turned, so that one might have thought it had been brought to the boil by the light of the moon.

There were six or eight of us, dumb-struck and full of wonder, our gaze fixed towards the unseen coast of Africa, for which we were bound. The captain, who was the guiding light of our party, was smoking a cigar when he took up once more the dinner-time conversation.

"Oh yes," he said, "I experienced fear that day all right. My ship had been stranded there for six hours with this rock driven into her belly, and lashed by heavy seas. Happily for us, as the light was failing, an English coaster spotted us and came to our aid."

At this point, a large man with a bronzed face and grave expression—one of those men who you feel has traversed great tracts of unknown territories in the midst of constant danger, and whose calm eyes seem to harbour in their depths some essence of the strange countries he has known; one of those men who is, one senses, steeped in deeds of derring do—chose to speak for the first time.

"You say, captain, that you have experienced fear. I feel inclined to doubt that; you are perhaps mistaken in your choice of word and in the description of the sensation you have experienced. An active healthy man does not feel afraid in the face of imminent danger. He is agitated perhaps, on the alert, even alarmed, but fear, that is something else."

The captain responded with a laugh. "Fiddlesticks! I tell you without reservation that I was afraid, no question!"

The man with the bronzed complexion spoke softly.

"Permit me to explain! Fear (and the bravest of men must feel fear), is something frightful; a horrific sensation, comparable to a complete disintegration of the spirit, an unspeakable fracture of thought and feeling, the memory of which alone gives rise to sensations of panic; but that does not occur when one is on guard, neither before an assault, nor before apparently certain death; nor when confronted with all known forms of peril. It occurs in abnormal circumstances, under certain mysterious conditions, and in the face of uncertain hazards. True fear is something like the recall of fantastical terrors of yesteryear. A man who believes in ghosts and can conceive of himself confronted by a spectre in the night, is capable of experiencing fear in all its unspeakable horror.

"Myself, I have felt fear in broad daylight, about ten years ago as a matter of fact; and I felt it again, last winter, one night in December.

"The truth is I have survived many dangers, many adventures that seemed mortal. I have been beaten up, more than once. I have been left for dead by robbers. I have been condemned as a rebel to be hanged in America, and been thrown into the sea off the coast of China. Each time I have believed myself lost, and have reconciled myself to my fate without any self-pity or even regrets. But that is not fear.

"I had sensed it in Africa, even though fear is truly a child of the north. The sun there can be as blinding in its effect as fog—take note of that gentlemen— amongst the Orientals life is cheap, one becomes resigned to that at once; the nights are clear and devoid of those uneasy shadows that haunt the brain in colder regions. In the east one can experience panic, but fear is unknown. Well then, here is what happened to me in this land of Africa:

"I was crossing the great dunes to the south of Ouargla. It is one of the world's strangest terrains— smooth sand, as endless as interminable ocean beaches. Now then, imagine the ocean itself has turned to sand during a storm; picture a silent tempest of turbulent peaks of yellow dust. They are mountainous, these unpredictable waves, diverse, raised up for all the world like untamed ocean billows, only higher, and streaked like marble. Onto this dumb and motionless raging ocean, the all-consuming southern sun directs its unfiltered and implacable heat. These inclines of golden ash must be ascended and descended, time after time, climbed without ceasing, without rest or shade. The horses simply floundered, sinking to their knees on the upslope then sliding down the other side of these successive unending hills.

"We were two companions accompanied by eight tribesmen, and four camels with their drivers. We no longer spoke, overcome by heat and tiredness and as parched with thirst as the burning desert itself. Suddenly, one of our company emitted a kind of cry. We all stopped at once, remaining motionless, startled by one of those inexplicable phenomena familiar to travellers in these God-forsaken places. Somewhere, near at hand, from an indeterminate direction, a drum was beating—the mysterious 'tambour' of the sand dunes—it was beating quite distinctly, sometimes more resonant, sometimes more faintly, stopping then resuming its fantastical refrain.

"The terrified Arabs looked at each other in alarm, and one said in their native tongue, 'Death is upon us'. Then all of a sudden, my companion, my friend, almost my brother, plunged head first from his horse, felled by sunstroke.

"And for two hours, during which time I tried in vain to save him, this incessant drumbeat filled my ears with its intermittent, incomprehensible and unearthly noise; and I felt, in my very bones, fear—true, hideous fear in the presence of this beloved cadaver, in this out of the way hole amidst four mountain peaks of burning sand inflamed by a pitiless sun, two hundred leagues from the nearest French speaking village and assailed by the insistent inexplicable echo of the rapidly beating drum.

"On that day, I understood what it was to feel fear, and I have felt it even more keenly on one other occasion ..."

The captain interrupted the speaker, "Excuse me sir, but this drum you speak of? What was it?"

"I have no idea, no one had. Officers, often surprised by this singular noise generally attribute it to a sound wave, magnified, multiplied, immeasurably inflated by the undulations of the sand dunes, or to a hail of sand particles carried on a gust of wind and striking a clump of dried grasses; for it is often remarked that the phenomenon produces in the vicinity little plants that are scorched by the sun and tough as parchment. This drum then would be a sort of sonic mirage, that is all; but of course, I learned all that much later.

"I come now to my second manifestation. It was

last winter, in a forest in north-eastern France. Nightfall arrived two hours early, such was the overcast condition of the sky. I had for a guide a peasant who walked at my side along a narrow path vaulted over by firs through which a wild wind was echoing. Above the treetops I could see clouds scurrying in disarray as though fleeing before some disaster. Sometimes under a fierce gust, the entire forest bent to one side with a cry of pain, and the chill struck through to the marrow despite my rapid pace and heavy clothing.

"We were going to sup and lodge with a warden whose house was not too far distant. I was going there to hunt.

"My guide, every now and then, raised his eyes and murmured: 'Sad times!' Then he spoke of the folk with whom we were going to stay. The father had killed a poacher two years previously and ever since he had been melancholic, as though haunted by the memory. His two sons, both married, resided with him.

"The shadows were impenetrable. I could see nothing, either before or around me, and all the interlaced tracery of the trees filled the night with an incessant clamour. At last I saw a light and very soon my companion was knocking at the door. Strident women's cries responded, followed by a man's constricted voice demanding: 'Who goes there?' My guide identified himself and we went in—what an unforgettable picture!

"An old man with white hair, wild eyes and a loaded gun in his hand was standing waiting for us in the middle of the kitchen, whilst two great louts armed with axes, guarded the door. I could just make out in the dark corners, two women on their knees, their faces hidden against the wall.

"Bear with me while I fill in the details. The old man replaced his firearm against the wall and ordered the preparation of my room; then, since the women did not budge, he addressed me gruffly, 'You see, Sir, I killed a man two years ago this very night. Last year he came back to call upon me. I await him again this evening.'

"Then he added in a tone that caused me to smile—'For this reason we are not quite ourselves.' I reassured him as best I could, curious as I was to have arrived that very evening in time to experience this superstitious terror. I would recount some tales of my own, presently, and perhaps succeed in calming everyone a little.

"Near the fireplace an old dog, almost blind and heavily bewhiskered, one of those dogs who reminds you of someone you know, was sleeping, his muzzle between his paws.

"Outside, the relentless storm was battering the little house, when suddenly, through a narrow square pane, a sort of spyhole placed next to the door, I saw a whole clump of trees bowled over by the wind, in the bright glare of great lightning flashes.

"Despite my efforts, I could keenly sense that a deep terror held these people in its grip, and each time I ceased talking, all ears were on the alert. To avoid being an eyewitness to those idiotic fears, I was going to request permission to retire, when suddenly the old man leapt from his chair, and, once more seizing his gun, stammered in a distracted voice, 'There he is! There he is! I can hear him!'

"The two women collapsed onto their knees in their respective corners hiding their faces, and the two sons again grabbed hold of their axes. I was, once again, about to attempt to calm them when the sleeping dog woke up suddenly; then, throwing up its head, extending its neck and looking towards the fire with its virtually sightless eyes it emitted one of those unearthly howls which put the fear of God into travellers, at dusk in the open countryside. All eyes turned towards him. Meanwhile he remained rooted to the spot, rigid on his four paws as though haunted by an unseen vision, and proceeded to howl in the direction of this invisible object—unfamiliar, frightful no doubt, for all his hairs were standing on end! The warden, agitated, cried out—'He sees him! He sees him! He was there when I killed him!' And the two women, wholly distraught, began howling in unison with the dog.

"Despite myself, a great shudder ran between my shoulder blades. This spectre of the animal in this place, at this hour, in the midst of these distracted people, was frightening to behold I tell you!

"For a whole hour, this dog howled without budging from the spot; he howled as in the anguish of a dream; and the frightful fear was transmitted to myself. Fear of what? Do I know? It was simply 'fear'. And there's an end of it.

"We remained motionless, panic-stricken in the expectation of a fearful happening, ears attentive, hearts pumping, ready to leap out of our skins at the slightest noise.

"Then the dog began prowling around the place sniffing the walls and whining constantly. This beast was driving us mad. Suddenly the peasant who had brought me here threw himself upon it in a sort of paroxysm of raging terror and, opening the door which gave onto the little courtyard, flung the animal outside.

"He shut up immediately, and we remained there plunged into an even more terrifying silence. Then, out of the blue, and all at one and the same time, we collectively experienced this communal shock.

"A being glided against the outside wall that faced the forest. Then it brushed against the door on which it seemed to knock with a tentative hand; then nothing more was heard for a further two minutes which to us seemed like an eternity; then it returned, feeling its way along the wall, scratching lightly as a child might do with its nail; then, horror of horrors, a head appeared against the pane of the spyhole, an entirely white head with eyes as luminous as those of wild beasts. And from its mouth an indecipherable sound, a plaintive moan. Then an ear-splitting noise resounded around the kitchen. The old warden had fired his gun and immediately the sons hastened to block up the spyhole upending the big table and placing it on top of the sideboard.

"And I swear to you that from the noise of the gunshot onwards, I was in such anguish of heart, soul and body, that I felt myself utterly undone and ready to die of fear.

"We remained there till dawn, incapable of moving, of saying a word, shrivelled and imprisoned within an inexpressible madness.

"No one dared to take down the barricade until a thin ray of daylight was seen through the slit of a shutter.

"At the foot of the outside wall, and stretched across the threshold, the old dog lay dead, its muzzle shattered by a bullet. He had got back into the yard by digging a hole under the palisade."

The man with the bronzed face went quiet, then he added, "That night, though at no time did I encounter any danger, I may tell you one thing—I would rather face once more all the real perils I have undergone in my travels, than relive the one minute that followed the shattering of the glass in that spyhole."

The Devil

Home And Away

This story, yet another from the pen of de Maupassant, is one of the earliest I remember encountering in the French language. The teacher who introduced us to it stressed the similarities between the harsh lifestyle of the 19th-century Norman peasant and the unrelenting calendar of the Ulster farmer of days gone by; and some years later I noted that affinity of spirit in many of the rustic dramas of the Co. Antrim playwright George Shiels. With their sharply drawn characters and uncompromising line on matters of life and death, the resemblance is sometimes startling. A young woman, for example, is described in very favourable terms as having a mouthful of teeth like a young horse and immeasurable strength in her arm; and when the central character of MacCook's Corner bullies a simple-minded man in his sixties into admitting that his domineering father is a man of ninety, the caustic response is: "It's time he wasn't here. Ye'll need tae tak' him up tae the top of a tall mountain, an' set him there till God sees him; or ye may hae tae shoot him in the end."

In my version of the story I have very much borne in mind the style of Shiels and in so doing changed the location and the names of the characters. In other respects, I have endeavoured where possible to be faithful to both the spirit and the letter of de Maupassant's text.

The Devil

The son stood facing the doctor at the foot of his mother's bed. Herself—calm, resigned and with all her wits about her—watched the two men impassively and listened to their discourse. She was going to die, she had no complaints, her time had come; she was ninety-two years of age.

The July sun streamed through the open door and window and on to the brown earthen floor, the strong rays shining on a smooth uneven surface rammed down hard by four generations of peasant clogs. The smell of the fields wafting in, borne on the warm breeze; odours of grass, wheat, leaves scorched in the noonday heat. Chirruping grasshoppers were filling the air with their toneless crake-like din, for all the world like the sound of wooden rattles sold to children at the fair.

The doctor, raising his voice, said, "Now then Michael James, you can't leave your mother all alone in this state. She could pop off at any moment."

"That's all well and good," said the farmer cautiously, "but what about my wheat? It's lying cut o'er long as it is, and besides, the weather's perfect. What do you say, ma?"

And the dying old woman, steeped to the last in peasant avarice, nodded and winked affirmatively, urging her son back to his wheatfield and implying she'd be perfectly capable of dying on her own.

The doctor put his foot down. "You're a heartless gossoon and that's a fact," said he, "but I'll not allow it! If you attending to your wheat takes precedence over looking after your dying mother, then hire Granny Greer to watch over her. God dammit, man, I insist! And if you don't do as I say, then, when your turn comes, I'll leave you to die like a dog. Am I making myself clear?" And with that parting shot, he left.

Granny Greer, an old crone who took in ironing, had also charge of the dead and dying of the surrounding districts. That said, as soon as she had wrapped her charges in the sheet they would never turn back, she would once more pick up her iron, and wield it to and fro upon the linen of the living. As wrinkled as an apple of yesteryear, she was spiteful, covetous, avaricious to a remarkable degree, and literally bent double, as though fractured at the hip from the constant movement of iron on cloth. She was, moreover, entirely and utterly obsessed by each and every aspect of death, for which she nutured in her ageing loins an obscene and morbid passion. Her sole conversation consisted of lingering over every lurid detail of deaths she had witnessed, recounting, *ad nauseam*, every nuance of the final agony; her tales never varying one iota, as the hunter will recall every kill.

When Michael James O'Gorman called on her, he found her tying up and dipping the blue bag that ensured the pristine whiteness of the village women's lace collars.

"Good afternoon," he said, "How are things with you?"

Turning her head slightly askance, she replied, "Fair to middling. Fair to middling—and yourself?"

"Oh, I'm well enough, its me ma that's not. She's about ready to give up the ghost, I'm thinking."

The old peasant woman removed her hands from the water whose droplets, blue-tinted and transparent, ran down to her finger tips and then back into the tub. She enquired with apparent concern, "As far gone as *that* is she?"

"The doctor says she'll not see out the afternoon."

"You're certain she's that bad?"

Michael James hesitated. He needed to prevaricate a bit before putting his proposition but since he could not find the words for small talk he came straight to the point—"How much would you charge me, all in?" he asked.

Granny Greer paused for a moment, then answered solemnly: "I have two rates. Two shillings per day and three shillings per night for the well-to-do; and for the others, a shilling for the daylight hours and two shillings from dusk till dawn. I'll charge you one shilling and two."

Michael James thought this over. He knew his old mother to be tenacious, wiry, and stubborn; she could last out a whole week despite the doctor's prognosis. "No," he said emphatically, "I'd prefer a set price from start to finish. I'll take my chance, one way or the other. The doctor says she'll go quickly. If that's the case then I'm the loser, but if she holds out to tomorrow or the next day then I reap the benefit."

The old skinflint looked at him in some surprise.

The Devil

She had never taken a gamble on death before. She paused for a moment, tempted by the thought of easy pickings; then she wondered if he might not be trying to put one over on her.

"I can't say till I've seen your mother," she countered cautiously.

"Then come and take a look," said he.

She wiped her hands and followed him at once. On the way, they did not exchange a single word. She walked quickly, her short legs taking two steps to his one; he loped along, as though crossing a stream at every stride. The cows, overcome by the heat and stretched full-length in the fields, raised their heads reluctantly—mooing mournfully as though to beg fresh grass from the passers-by. Nearing the house, Michael James O'Gorman murmured softly, "If it's all over, well and good, so be it," the hopeful tone of his voice betraying his subconscious wish.

But the old lady was *not* dead. She lay on her back in the truckle bed, her hands on the purple counterpane—hands that were dreadfully thin and gnarled, as though of some unearthly crab-like creature, curled up cruelly by arthritis and the hard life and daily toil of nigh on a century. Granny Greer approached the bed and assessed the dying woman. She took her pulse, tapped her chest, and listened to her breathing; questioned her in order to hear her speak, then, after due deliberation, she left the room, followed by Michael James. She had reached the conclusion that the old woman would not make it till nightfall.

"Well, what's the verdict?" he asked, and the old rascal replied, "She'll last a good two days, likely three; you'll give me six shillings all inclusive."

"Six shillings!" he protested. "Are you clean off your head? We'll be lucky if she lasts six hours!"

And so they disputed and haggled at length, each unwilling to budge an inch; but she, threatening to walk off—precious time going by and the wheat unforked where it lay—your man at last gave way. "Right," he said, exasperated, "Six shillings and no extras—the body boxed and ready for burial."

"Six shillings it is," said she. He at once marched off to attend to his harvest, heading towards the grain which was still spread out under a pitiless sun.

Granny Greer went back inside. She had brought her sewing with her, for all the while she watched over the dying and the dead she worked without ceasing, either for herself, or in order to exact a bonus from the bereaved family, thus supplementing the fees due to her. On a sudden impulse, she enquired, "I take it you've had the last sacraments, Mrs. O'Gorman?" The old lady shook her head and Granny Greer, who was very devout, leapt to her feet. "Blessed Lord above, it's not possible! I'll go fetch the priest." So saying, she fled from the room and rushed towards the presbytery at such a rate that the urchins in the square, noting the great haste, concluded that there had been an accident.

The priest responded at once, hurriedly donning his vestments and dashing out of doors with the sacraments, preceded by an altar boy ringing a little bell to announce God's passage through the quiet, sun-baked parish. Men, working some distance away, removed their broad-brimmed bonnets till the white-robed priest disappeared from view; women gathering sheaves stood and made the sign of the cross; startled black hens scuttled along dry ditches till they found the familiar hole in the hedge, then vanished without trace; a colt tied up in a paddock, bolted at the sight of the surplice, and galloped pell-mell at the end of its tether, bucking and kicking frantically. The choirboy in his crimson cassock trotted onward, and the priest, his head on one side and holding on to his square biretta, followed after, muttering prayers, with Granny Greer hindmost, bent double as though trying to prostrate herself and run at the same time, her hands tightly clasped as though in church. From afar, Michael James observed their passing and enquired, "Where's the priest off to, then?" His farm labourer, more worldly wise than he, replied, "No doubt he'll be taking the last rites to your mother."

"Indeed! Like as not!" said your man, not turning a hair, and at once resumed his work. Mother O'Gorman made her confession, received absolution, and took communion. Then the priest went off, leaving the women alone.

Granny Greer began to weigh up the dying woman's chances. How long was this going to take? Daylight was failing. Cooler air was entering the house and a stiffer breeze was rustling a seaside postcard pinned to the wall, making it flap up and down. The little window curtains, at one time white, but now yellow with age and spattered with flies, fluttered frantically as though trying to break free, anxious to be off and away like the old lady's soul.

Stock still, eyes wide open, she seemed to be utterly resigned to the death that was so near, yet so long in coming. Her breathing, short and whistling feebly in her constricted throat, would stop in due course, and the world would be minus one woman, whom nobody would miss.

At nightfall, Michael James returned, and approaching the bed, saw that his mother was still alive. "How d'you feel?" he asked, as he always did when she was poorly; then he sent Granny Greer home, calling out after her: "Five o'clock on the dot," and sure enough, she arrived at the crack of dawn. Michael James was eating his homemade gruel before setting off for the fields. "Well," asked the crone, "has your mother passed over?" and he, with a malevolent glint replied, "She's slightly improved if anything." Then he was gone.

Twenty-four hours elapsed; she had stayed overnight—still no change. Michael James once more set off for the fields and still the old lady lay there, short of breath, inscrutable, eyes wide open, hands still clasped above the quilt. She was now into her third day! It might take another three or four, even a week! Things were getting desperate; panic seized old

Greer's miserly breast, and fury rose in her gorge at this man who had outwitted her, and this stubborn old witch who refused to die. Sullenly, she set to work and waited, her gaze fixed on the wizened face of her charge. Michael James showed up at lunchtime, well pleased with himself, even smug. Then back he went to work with a will. Conditions outdoor were excellent.

Mother Greer was reaching breaking point. Each minute that went by now seemed like stolen labour, stolen cash. She felt a mad urge to grab this obstinate, headstrong old wretch by the throat and with the merest squeeze to terminate this shallow breathing which was robbing her of time and money; but then she thought of the risk and other, more plausible ideas entering her head, she approached the bed and asked slyly, "Have you seen the Devil yet?"

"No," replied the old woman feebly.

"Ah, well ... " said Granny Greer, moving closer and whispering malevolently into Mrs. O'Gorman's ear— and there and then she began making up stories designed to scare the old lady to death—

"A matter of minutes before they expire," she began, "the Devil appears to all who are at death's door. He has a broom in his fist, a pot on his head and he lets out loud, unearthly shrieks. Once you have seen him it's all over; you have only seconds left—in fact, the sooner you depart, the better!"

Then she enumerated all those women to whom the Devil had appeared that very year, exactly at the point of death—she herself had seen him each time— Josie Mooney, Ellie McCrory, Sophie Patterson and so on.

The stories finally began to register with the old dame who fidgeted nervously, wringing her hands and twisting her head, trying to peer into the farthest corners of the room. Suddenly, Greer disappeared and from a cupboard she took a sheet, in which she draped herself from head to toe. She then placed over her head the coal black cooking pot, from which three bowed feet protruded like devil's horns and, seizing a broom in her right hand and, in her left, an enamel pail, she flung the latter into the air so that it fell to earth with the most almighty clatter, echoing and re-echoing horribly. Whereupon, she mounted a chair and, parting the drape at the foot of the bed, she made a sudden appearance, waving her arms about wildly, emitting fearsome cries from within the pot, brandishing the broom like the Devil in the Punch and Judy show. Terrified beyond endurance, her eyes wide open in sheer horror, the dying old lady made a frantic, nay superhuman, effort to rise up and flee. She actually managed to raise her shoulders and withered shanks clear of the mattress, before falling back with a profound sigh. It was all over.

Old Greer calmly put everything back in its place, the broom against the corner of the cupboard, the sheet inside it, the cooking pot in the hearth, the bucket on the shelf and the chair against the wall. Then, with professional expertise, she closed the corpse's staring eyes, placed a bowl on the bed and poured out the holy water. Then, kneeling down, she piously set about reciting the prayers for the dead which, as part of her trade, she knew by heart. Everything else was swiftly done and in excellent order—the body scrubbed, stretched, laid out, and into the winding sheet ... When, come evening, Michael returned, he heard the prayers and deduced at once that she had gained a whole shilling on him; for she had watched over his mother for three days and one night only, which came to just five shillings, whereas he, the fool, had settled for six.

The Umbrella

Home And Away

This study of an obsessively thrifty bourgeois housewife is another De Maupassant classic, and it transfers very readily to a genteel Belfast 'faubourg'. I have brought the story forward in time to within the period of my own childhood memories—let us imagine it to be the Spring of 1940—when one or two ladies of that nature etched their personalities on my receptive brain cells. I have re-named her 'Jeanie McIvor', though I hasten to add that it is entirely fictitious; any McIvors that I have known have been the soul of generosity, and any resemblance to a member of that excellent clan, be they quick or be they deceased, is pure coincidence. I should imagine the family residence to have been located somewhere in the Belmont, or Upper Newtownards Road areas, though it could just as readily have been Rosetta, or Ravenhill; that of course would conveniently increase the tram fares to Stormont.

The Umbrella

She was just a wee slip of a woman—forty years of age and five foot nothing—neat as ninepence, forever on guard, with puckered mouth and furrowed brow and grumpy more often than not. Her husband never ceased complaining of the restraints she imposed upon him, all the more hurtful because they wounded his vanity. He was a head clerk in the Civil Service at Stormont when the war broke out—something to do with the Defence Ministry—and remained there past retirement age at his wife's insistence, for no better reason than to boost their already adequate resources.

Thrift was second nature to Mrs. McIvor. She knew the value of a copper, and had a whole arsenal of proverbial sayings to back up her innate canniness: 'Look after the pennies ...', 'Put something by for a rainy day', and so on.

Her daily woman had to account for every brass farthing and her husband's pocket money was kept to the bare minimum. To tell the truth, they were quite comfortably off, having no children to support but with Mrs. Jeanie McIvor the hoarding of money was an illness, an obsession—parting with a bit of loose change made her physically sick—and every single expenditure, however necessary, gave rise to a sleepless night. John McIvor was forever saying to his spouse: "You shouldn't be so near, Jeanie" —a nice and precise example of an Ulster-Scots dialect word—but she would predictably return his fire with a double-barrelled blast from her aforesaid arsenal of maxims: "You never know what's round the corner.", "It's better to be safe than sorry!"

For the past year or so, Mr. McIvor had been turning up at the office with the same old patched-up brolly affording endless amusement to his junior associates. Finally driven to distraction by their leg-pulling, he put his foot down and insisted his wife should purchase a new one. In fact she procured a cut-price, mass-produced effort from Woollies for a mere pittance; but when his colleagues caught sight of this latest eyesore which was duplicated all over town like a cheap imitation of a circus parasol, or a fancy dress accessory from Elliots' Joke Shop, they positively fell about with glee, causing poor Mr. McIvor even more acute embarrassment. The article was a complete washout and in no time at all was in such a state of disrepair that the laughter in the building was causing pandemonium with the whole edifice resounding from morn till night with a raucous parody of the old music hall song: "Any umber-ellas, any umber-ellas to mend today ..."("I've a feeling John McIvor's umber-ella's coming my way ...")

Driven to his wit's end, poor Mr. McIvor finally cracked and gave his wife an ultimatum; either she bought him a brand new gentleman's gamp from Robinson & Cleaver—silk covered and costing at least one guinea—or he would take a tram to work, there and back every day, thereby adding two shillings a week to their expenditure. In fact she compromised and obtained one from the Bank Buildings for fourteen and eleven pence. Flushed with vexation she thrust it at her husband, saying, "There you are, that should see you out!"

—Meaning I suppose that he wouldn't see another one this side of the grave. Be that as it may, the bold Mr. McIvor was transformed overnight from a miserable flop to an instant success. The new gamp silenced the office jokers and no doubt sowed the seeds of envy in uncharitable hearts. Returning home that evening however, McIvor and his brand new acquisition were given a quick once over by the ever watchful wife who promptly began to nag, "You're not going to leave it with that elastic cutting into the silk? Undo it for heaven's sake! You'd better take good care of it, do you hear, for I'm not buying another in the foreseeable future ..."

So saying, she snatched it from him, unfastening the ring and shaking out the pleats. Instantly she was rooted to the spot as though she had seen a ghost. A round hole the size of a florin—evidently a cigar burn—presented itself to her gaze right in the centre of one of the panels. For once, she was almost lost for words, but managed to stammer: "Wha ... what's happened?"

"Happened to what?" her husband replied coolly, not bothering to look.

Anger all but choked her, very nearly removing the power of speech altogether.

"You ... you ..." she spluttered, "You've burnt a ... a hole ... a hole in your ... umbrella! That's what's happened! You ... you ... Are you clean off your head? Are you trying to ruin us?"

Feeling himself turn deathly pale, he faced her for the first time. "What are you saying?"

"What am I saying ...? I'm saying you've scorched a hole in your brand new umbrella, that's what! Look!"

Then charging forward as though to strike him, she thrust the damaged article under his nose, displaying the gaping hole. Forced to examine the 'injury' at close quarters he was virtually poleaxed.

"That's ... that's not ... well, what, what is it? I don't know ..."

"Don't know? Don't know?" she screeched.

"I've done nothing, I swear to God. I haven't a notion how it got in that state."

She was yelling now at the top of her voice: "Oh, I dare say you've been acting the goat at work, opening and closing it in all directions—showing off—"

"I opened it once to show them what good quality silk it was. That's the God's honest truth."

But she was positively sizzling with rage now, and laid into him hammer and tongs, staging one of those scenes of marital disharmony that can turn the domestic hearth into something resembling the Battle of the Boyne; obviously her armoury of truisms did not include the one that says 'Least said soonest mended.'

Though talking of which she spent the rest of the evening in total silence patching the hole with a piece of fabric from the old umbrella, which was of a remarkably different shade. Next morning Mr. McIvor much subdued, set off with his renovated weather cover and hid it away in an office cupboard, putting it out of sight and out of mind, in much the same way as an unwelcome thought is banished from memory.

Returning home was a different kettle of fish altogether. No sooner had he stepped into the hall than Mrs. McIvor once more grabbed hold of the gamp, opening it out to check its state of health. Horror of horrors! It was now pitted with tiny perforations as though someone had tipped the contents of a still smouldering pipe all over it. The umbrella was done for, damaged beyond recall.

She surveyed the wreckage in stony silence, too appalled to utter a single word. Not a murmur escaped from her trembling lips; he too, gawped wordlessly at the disastrous spectacle—stupefied, dismayed and dumbfounded. They caught each other's eye momentarily but he averted his gaze; then, wham! He was struck full in the face by the now redundant luxury item which she had flung at him with some force, rediscovering her voice in a frenzy of abuse. "You clown! You scum! You half-wit! You did this on purpose—but I'll make you pay, you'll not get another—"

And so on, for what seemed like an eternity. When the storm finally abated, he tried to tell his side of the story: he hadn't the foggiest notion how it had happened. Maybe someone had it in for him; it was done out of envy, or in spite; some junior he had ticked off was getting his own back ...

The situation was saved by a knock at the door. She had almost forgotten. A friend had been invited to high tea, a solicitor's clerk as luck would have it. Mrs. McIvor, outwardly calm, set the facts before him as she set the table, concluding that buying another umbrella was clean out of the question.

The friend countered reasonably that such a decision could lead to ruined clothing and so incur even more expense; still inwardly seething, the little spitfire hit back—"In that case, he can have a cheap second-hand one and none of your silk either!"

That did it, John McIvor, for once boiled over. "Very well, Jeanie, I'll just have to hand in my notice.

I'm not showing up at the Ministry with a tatty umbrella. It would be unpatriotic—disloyal."

The friend tried to placate matters: "How about having it recovered?"

"That could cost as much as eight shillings! Or seven and six at least!" said Jeanie McIvor, adding forcefully, "Eight plus fifteen makes twenty-three. Twenty-three shillings in all for a patched-up umbrella. It's unthinkable; completely out of the question!"

The friend, himself a man of modest means, suddenly had a brainwave—"What about insurance?"

It took a few moments for this to sink in, as the friend added, "It could come under fire damage, if the accident occurred in the home; a little white lie perhaps?"

Jeanie McIvor picked up the point at once and immediately turned to her husband:

"Call in at the first opportunity, John. Report the damage and make a claim; it's simply a matter of filling in a form."

"I'd not have the brass neck and besides, it's dishonest," said Mr. McIvor.

"It's not like it's a month's salary! Let's keep a sense

of proportion shall we—there's not been a death in the family"—and with that the discussion ground to a halt. The following morning, John McIvor set off for the office wielding a walking stick, fortunately the weather was fine.

Left alone with her thoughts, Jeanie McIvor could not come to terms with the loss of her fifteen shillings. She had placed the umbrella in the centre of her spacious kitchen and after walking around it several times had still reached no firm conclusion. The prospect of the insurance money gladdened her little heart but the daunting prospect of convincing some po-faced clerk of the justice of her claim scared the wits out of her. She was shy and reserved with strangers, blushed at the slightest thing and lost her tongue in the presence of people she did not know.

To set against all that, there was the sad loss of money; it almost amounted to a bereavement of sorts, or heartache at the very least. The hours went by but the pain and sense of loss got no better. Then suddenly her spirits lifted, her mind was made up; she'd have a go and see what transpired.

First of all, however, she'd have to make a good job of the fire damage and put her claim beyond question.

She took a box of Swift matches from the mantelpiece and burned a hole as big as her husband's fist between the two spokes. Then she rolled up the charred remnant and fastened it with elastic. Putting on her hat and coat, she went to the end of the avenue and caught a tram for Castle Junction, just around the corner from Royal Avenue where the insurance company had their premises. Getting off the tram and crossing the road she slackened pace to almost a standstill, wondering what to say, imagining their reactions.

Turning into Royal Avenue itself, she examined the numbers on the buildings and realised she still had some way to go—another block perhaps—it gave her some time to consider; but suddenly she was there! On a massive oak door in letters of gold were written: INTERNATIONAL INSURANCE COMPANY

Daunted somewhat she dilly-dallied, shilly-shallied and shambled back and forth like a hermit crab in a quandary. Finally, taking her courage in both hands she told herself sternly that she must enter and sooner rather than later. Just the same, as she stepped inside, she was aware that her little heart was thumping, ten to the dozen.

She came to a large room with cubicles all around, in each cubicle a man's head could be seen through a grill, the rest of the body hidden by a panelled frame. A man appeared carrying a large file. She stopped and asked him in a tiny timid voice, "Excuse me but could you please tell me where I should enquire about claims concerning fire damage?"

His voice boomed out: "Disasters is what you want. First floor, on the left."

The dreaded word undermined her confidence and her immediate instinct was to run away, say no more and kiss good-bye to her fifteen shillings but the thought of that—to her—substantial sum, stiffened her resolve somewhat and so she began to mount the stairs, with an intake of breath on every step.

To her left she saw a door on which she tapped and a brisk voice called out, "Enter."

She found herself in an airy, well-appointed room where three rather self-important men were talking quietly but earnestly amongst themselves. One of them turned to her politely and asked, "How can I help you, madam?"

She froze within but managed to whisper in a small squeaky voice, "I've ... I've come about a disaster."

The man was extremely civil.

"Just take a seat, madam and I'll be with you in a moment,"

Then, turning to the others he continued his discussion. "The company, gentlemen, estimates its liability in your case at no more than twenty thousand pounds. We feel obliged to oppose your claim for a further five thousand pounds which is considerably above the original agreed assessment ..."

The other two men politely agreed to differ. In that case, they thought, perhaps the courts should arbitrate. With that, they took their leave and departed. "Such sums of money", she thought and wished the ground would open up and swallow her but the man had returned and asked what her problem was.

"I've come about this," said she in a feeble voice, unfurling after several abortive attempts the skeletal umbrella with bits of tattered silk clinging to the frame like shreds of shrivelled skin. The man half-closed his eyes as though in sympathy.

"It looks in a parlous state and that's a fact".

"I paid twenty guineas for it", said she.

"Really! As much as that?"

The Umbrella

"It was a quality product. My husband works at Stormont ... for the Ministry of Defence."

Perhaps this impressed the man, who was himself a humble air-raid warden in his spare time ... At all events he seemed to soften a bit. What he could not grasp, however, was what exactly he was to do about it. She pressed on: "It is fire damage. You can see it has been burnt."

"Oh yes. I can see that all right."

She sat open-mouthed for a moment, unsure how to continue. She'd obviously started off on the wrong foot but she quickly pulled herself together. "My name is Mrs. McIvor—Mrs. John McIvor and we are insured with your company against fire and theft; I have come to make a claim."

Thinking suddenly that she might have gone too far, she added, "I want you to have it recovered, that is all."

The manager, sensing a weakness, countered sharply, "But, madam, this is not an umbrella repair shop. We cannot undertake work of that sort."

Jeanie McIvor took this as a challenge. She could sense that the man was getting out of his depth, whilst she herself was gaining ground; she resolved to make a fight of it.

"I simply wish to claim for the cost of repairs. I could if need be undertake the work myself; but allow me to inform you that only last December we had a chimney fire causing over fifty pounds worth of damage, yet Mr. McIvor chose on that occasion to make no claim."

Detecting a falsehood, the manager said with a smile, "You must admit it's a bit odd that your husband failed to make application for substantial fire damage and now you are asking for a trifling sum to repair a worn out umbrella."

"Oh, not worn out, damaged by fire", said the lady sweetly.

"The fact is, that the cost of the chimney fire came out of Mr. McIvor's bank account whilst the umbrella comes out of Mrs. McIvor's household budget; and that is the difference—"

She was gaining the upper hand, no doubt about it—

"Just tell me the whole story," said the manager resignedly, as, sensing victory, she began.

"Well, at home we have in the hall this umbrella stand with, above it, this little shelf for candles and matches—we have electricity of course, but because of the blackout you understand"—

Yes, the manager understood.

"Anyway, the other day I struck three matches in succession and nothing happened."

"I take it they were utility matches," said the manager, making a joke of it.

"Oh, not at all. They were Maguire and Patterson's best pre-war Swift matches but perhaps they were damp. Anyway, the fourth match did the trick and I lit the candle, taking it up the stairs in its holder. There could have been a spark, for fifteen minutes later I could smell burning. Now I have a thing about fire, so ..."

She was obviously going to ramble on but the manager had heard enough, further resistance was, he concluded, 'not worth the candle'.

"What is your estimate of the damage?" he asked the suddenly speechless Mrs. McIvor.

Pulling herself together she was at pains to meet him halfway: "May I leave it with you to arrange the repairs?"

"Quite impossible, madam, just give me a figure."

"But I have no wish to take advantage. May I

suggest ... would it be acceptable to have the maker recover the umbrella in good quality silk, something durable and then pass the bill to you?"

"Perfectly acceptable, madam. Here is a note of hand for the cashier who will refund your money on presentation of a receipt."

He presented Mrs. McIvor with a signed authorisation and she, accepting the note with thanks, left hastily lest he should change his mind.

With lightsome step she crossed the High Street into Cornmarket and just off Ann Street she found a high class umbrella-maker. She marched right in and said with a confident air, "I would like this umbrella recovered in finest quality silk, the very best you have, regardless of the cost."

Master Manole

Home And Away

I looked at the name, and it registered 'Malone', as in 'Molly Malone', or 'Malone Road'; maybe it was a touch of dyslexia, or just blurred vision. I blinked, and the word became 'Maloney', so I reached for my glasses. I was standing before a painting in the National Gallery of Bucharest. It was an oil by Theodorescu-Sion, and it portrayed peasant women in rather monumental poses balancing pitchers on their heads, grouped around a formal covered fountain with a rounded arch, and set among a grove of trees. It was obviously some sort of shrine or meeting place, and the figures in the background were crowding around the spring itself which presumably had therapeutic as well as thirst-quenching properties. Clothes laid out on the grass, and a large basket in the foreground suggested that laundry was another activity. The painting's title was in fact, 'The Fountain of Manole', the final 'e' being pronounced.

I very soon discovered that the tradition surrounding this fountain is linked to one of Romania's most enduring legends, and the subject of an epic ballad which appears in many forms, though its geographical location is invariably Curtea de Arges, a former capital of Wallachia, or Muntenia as it was previously known. It concerns the building of the great Monastery Church which contains the tombs of the Romanian royal family. Much altered and 'improved upon' over the years, doubtless because of the royal associations, it was apparently first completed in 1526. Its founder was Prince Neagoe Basarab, as a rather sumptuous votive painting of the prince and his family displayed in the interior proclaims. Now, the hero or anti-hero of the ballad is Master Manole, a master builder or chief stonemason whose patron and overlord is called Negru-Voda, or Black Prince—generally thought to be the Prince Basarab portrayed in the painting, though this seems highly improbable. In fact this prince invited the Patriarch and all the fathers superior of Mount Athos in Greece to the dedication, as was recorded by Paul of Aleppo who visited the church in the following century, and who goes on to say, "Its late founder drained his heart's blood to have it built and did not spare any sum of money for its magnificence and decoration."

In the ballad, the opening ceremony is a downright disaster, a débâcle which was unlikely to have passed unnoticed in such distinguished company. However, the burning desire to build the biggest, the tallest, the finest monastic church on earth may well have pre-dated its fulfilment by a century or so.

Home And Away

The exploits of another Basarab in the year 1330 make him a more likely candidate. This prince, a thorn in the flesh of the Hungarian ruler and known to his enemies variously as Bazard, Bozarad, or even, who knows, 'Bozo', secured by his wiliness as much as by his skill in battle, the independence of the Romanian feudal state between the Carpathians and the Danube, and was therefore the founder of the Muntenian dynasty. Was this not a reason to erect a vast edifice?—a modern Romanian ruler showed such a weakness for large scale buildings—and besides, old 'Baz' was accused by his enemies, because he had attacked them whilst under his solemn promise of safe conduct, of being 'a mere cheat at good faith', a trait most admirably demonstrated by the prince in the ballad.

All this is pure conjecture of course. The facts are lost in the mists of time, though the moral of the story has at least one eternal truth enshrined in its telling: "Put not your trust in princes or kings."

Perhaps there are a couple of others: 'Don't make promises you cannot keep.'

And, above all: 'Don't ask your wife to bring your lunch to work.'

Here is the tale in English, recounted in prose, with

Master Manole

outbursts in ballad metre occurring from time to time. I have resisted the temptation to transfer the setting from Romania to the Boyne Valley and its associations with the ancient Kings of Ireland—to me the tale is essentially rooted by the banks of its own Carpathian stream. My initial lexical blunder has, however, bestowed a Hibernian surname on the chief protagonist; after all, Irish builders, like publicans, crop up in the oddest places—hence 'Gaffer Maloney'. I shall begin the story in the time-honoured way ...

Master Manole

One upon a time—a very long time—in a palace hard by the banks of the river Argesh, (that is how it is pronounced) there lived a black prince whose name was Bazarab, or Bazard ...

One fine morning in May he emerged from his palace and began walking purposefully up the river, plunged deep in thought and yet at the same time apparently on the alert as he darted sharp looks to his left and his right—carefully scanning both banks of the stream. Struggling somewhat behind, yet keeping up after a fashion, maintaining, so to speak, a discreet but not over-familiar proximity, was a group of ten men, artisans obviously and not courtiers, judging from their garb; they were in fact masons, nine journeymen and one master mason—the gaffer, Maloney. The prince stopped and started, paused here and there before proceeding further up the valley, then came to a halt in a more positive manner ensuring that the men gathered round, which they did, bareheaded and open-mouthed. The prince looked them up and down imperiously and then addressed them; it was the first time he had spoken.

"I am looking," said he, "for a spot that's divine, where a prince such as I might set up a shrine."

He impressed upon them that it was not any old place he was looking for, but an exact location that was clearly pictured in his mind's eye:

> "It's a vision that's locked in my brain," said the
> prince
> "An old rotting wall that's forgotten long since
> On a sward that is green, on a slope that is lush
> And hidden away in a thick hazel bush."

Just then a bold young shepherd boy strode past.

> "Your highness," says he, "such a bush have I seen
> And under it hides a wall rotting and green;
> My dogs cock their legs and then hurry away
> For the old wall is haunted, so country folk say."

At that, the prince fairly rushed to the wall, with Maloney in tow and the nine journeymen in pursuit.

Master Manole

Raising his eyes heavenward, he acknowledged that
Divine Providence had led him to this sacred spot:

Says the prince to Maloney, "Here is my wall
And I obligate you, as I obligate all —
Here do I choose to set up my shrine,
Here you must build me that cloister divine—

"A monastic foundation, that's what I desire.
An Episcopal church with a very tall spire,
And if you can make it the finest on earth
You'll very soon find what my gratitude's worth.

"For gold coins and silver will be your reward
And each of you men I'll turn into a lord;
But if you should fail me, or if you should falter,
The fate that awaits you 'll be worse than a halter."

And so they set to work, there and then, laying out
the site with rope and chain, digging foundations, a
ditch and a drain, toiling day and night, raising walls
that were both upright and stout. When they did
break off to rest and sleep, however, everything fell
down in a heap—day one, day two, day three, day

four, and every successive night reduced their handiwork to a pile of stones. The gaffer at first was sore perplexed, but after a week he was at his wit's end. Basra, tolerant to begin with, turned nasty, and swore to have them, for their trouble, buried beneath their pile of rubble; and so they tried harder; but poor Boss Maloney, meanwhile, was slowly losing his marbles —

On summer's days they'd toil and sweat
From daybreak till the sun had set;
Maloney, meanwhile, took to bed,
And lay there senseless, as one dead.

One minute he'd be counting sheep,
The next he'd nod off, half-asleep;
But long before the night was spent,
Oh, what a vivid dream he'd dreamt!

Yes, long before daybreak he sent for his dejected crew to tell them about his startling vision and appraise them of his desperate decision: "Gather around men," said the gaffer, "I know there's not a shirker among you, so rest assured I'm not looking for a scapegoat." Well, they heaved a sigh of relief, one and all, for inwardly their self-esteem was low. Meanwhile they listened, all agog, to hear the gaffer's master plan. "There's a curse on our work, it's as simple as that," said he, "and it will not improve, it can only get worse, so listen carefully:

"In my dream an inner voice
Cried, Boss Maloney, you've no choice,
You and your men an oath will swear
And stick to it, I do declare"—

Well, you could have heard a pebble drop —

"Whoever's wife, or sister dear,
Tomorrow morning doth appear,
Her, with haste, you must immure
And that will prove the certain cure.

"Brother, husband, come what may,
Must his dear one vow to slay;
Someone's sister, someone's wife,
He must tomorrow take her life!"

There was consternation at first, but each man, an

optimist at heart, thought to himself "It's unlikely to be me," and when Maloney reassured them that he was included in the oath, they all consented; and after all, old Bazard had promised them a fate worse than death if they did not complete the job.

Dawn arrived, the sun arose. Maloney stood on tiptoe. Still not espying anything amiss, he shimmied up the scaffolding:

Oh, what a vision met his gaze,
Peering through the morning haze;
For, sure it was his Anna dear,
Bearing bread and home-brewed beer.

Oh, yes, it was his bonny bride
Hasting to her husband's side;
His faithful Anna, sweet and good,
Her basket filled with wholesome food.

Hurrying to greet her spouse
In floral skirt and snow-white blouse.

The poor man fell to his knees and implored all the heavenly powers to come to his aid—"Dear God, send a cloud, let it pour torrential rain to turn my dear wife home again! Let it flood the Argesh river, that my sweet spouse may not cross over!"

The good Lord heard his prayer and sent down such a fearsome shower that the river burst its banks, the muddy waters swirling round poor Anna's flanks; but her sturdy peasant legs ploughed on and on, until scrambling up a handy ridge, she found a well-made wooden bridge:

"Oh, Lord above, send me a gale
That in her duty she may fail;
Oh, send a wind to turn her face
Away from this accursed place!"

And so the Lord sent down a wind
That made the fir trees creak and bend,
That made the maples sigh and moan,
Yet still brave Anna soldiered on—

Her shoulders high, her head held low,
She fended off each gusty blow,
And smiling through the stormy blast,
She reached her husband's arms, at last!

When brave Anna did appear
The men raised such a lusty cheer;
But poor Maloney was cast down,
All he could muster was a frown

As, clasping his sweet trusting missus,
He covered her with fearful kisses,
Then led her up a little stair
And stood her in a crevice there.

"Dear turtle dove, here is your nest,
I'll build it up for you in jest,
Then as I work, this motley crew
Can watch us as we two bill and coo."

Anna laughed at such a game, but the gaffer was
downright melancholic—she teased him as he plied
the trowel, "Hey, grumpy guts, why the scowl?"

"I'm doing this," he told her, "to bring a certain
dream to life"—she little dreamt he'd sworn an oath
that would, in fact, destroy them both; as the mortar
rose round pretty ankles, calves and thighs, poor
Anna's laughter turned to sighs, her smiles to
agonising cries:

"Maloney, oh my dear Maloney,
Pray give over your baloney;
This boorish jest has gone too far
This rough cement my flesh will mar."

But he worked on without a word,
Raising the walls up like a shroud;
Around her belly, breasts and shoulders,
He built that deadly nest of boulders:

"Maloney dearest, cease this madness
Your game has filled my heart with sadness
This wall, these stones, they weigh like lead:
You've crushed my baby, now it's dead!"

The babe was trapped within the womb and now
her belly was its tomb, but crazed Maloney closed his
ears to sobs and anguished tears, mortaring up her
comely breasts, her lips, eyes and all the rest, what
remained was just the moan:

"Maloney, oh, Maloney ..."

Just then, there appeared in view round a bend in

the river, the Black Prince and his retinue—lay, clergy, boyars, bishops—arriving in solemn procession for the consecration. What sumptuous pageantry! What a sight to behold—the flags aloft, the banners hung, as bells were rung and mass was sung. Women dancing on the green, the men lined up on the roof waving garlands of leaves—as pretty a picture as ever was seen. His Highness approaching knelt in prayer before this church so fine and rare. Maloney watched with bated breath and grieved for Anna's cruel death.

The prince arose and addressed the men who were formally lined up along the eaves:

"Tell me, worthy gentlemen, could you for my heart's desire erect for me another spire? A bigger one, a better one, the tallest spire in Christendom? Consider well your answer. Cross your heart and hope to die." The men puffed up with pride at their achievement did not hesitate: "Sure we'll build a bigger, better, follow your order to the letter—a longer nave, a loftier tower—whatever you require."

Prince Bassarab turned aside and brooded, his lips pursed, his eyes hooded: "This church they can improve upon, without so much as a second thought?" All eyes were on His Highness as he continued to ponder. The masons except for Maloney grinned broadly in anticipation of further employment, but Bazard's expression, as well as his countenance was blacker than black—all things considered. Maloney and his journeymen had let him down, given him second best—"These men aren't worth their salt," he muttered, in an offhand way. "Remove that scaffolding and lay those ladders on the ground," he ordered, "and leave those worthless masons up there to rot and die."

Each journeyman in disbelief
Stood there quaking like a leaf;
Then, when the awful truth sunk in,
Those workers kicked up such a din.

Seeking to avoid their fate
By making wings from bits of slate,
They closed their eyes and held their breath
Ere leaping off to certain death.

The bodies, as they hit the ground, made a most awful popping noise, guts, gore, and severed heads spattering the flower beds. Meanwhile, poor Maloney

standing there lonely and forlorn, braced himself on a
dizzy ledge and aimed towards a distant hedge,
hoping should he clear the outer wall, that it might
break his fall—a forlorn hope, it was a full furlong off!

Just then, a whisper sweet and low
Filtered up from far below—
The gaffer poised, a man apart—
This sound must surely break his heart!

"Maloney-oh, Maloney-oh"—
The voice was mournful, full of woe—
"This wall is as a ton of lead,
My womb is crushed, my baby's dead."

As Anna's murmurs reached his ears
The gaffer's eyes were drowned in tears;
Earth and sky spun upside down,
The clouds careering round and round.

Maloney leapt into the air
To crash to earth he knew not where
But where he fell—oh, wondrous thing—
From out of the ground, there gushed a spring!

Master Manole

Those doleful waters cured the gout
Attracting folk from miles about;
Disorders of the eyes and ears
Were washed in Boss Maloney's tears—

Some say that after all these years, that spring is still
the gaffer's tears; and while cynics will tell you that is
all baloney, it is still 'The Fountain of Maloney', or,
should I say Manole—anyway, it was all 'a very long
time ago'.

Three Dreams

The cautious Shorter Oxford Dictionary *definition of Dream (in its non figurative sense) seems to me perhaps just a touch too concise to conjure up that fantastical otherworld that awaits us beyond the gates of sleep. Since, however, it is a private and entirely subjective world, open to as much wild speculation and contentious argument as the afterlife, or our still confused notions of body and spirit, it may be wise to use it as a point of reference: 'A train of thoughts, images, or fancies passing through the mind during sleep; a vision during sleep; the state in which this occurs.'*

Vision, in this context incidentally, is defined in the same dictionary as 'Something which is apparently seen otherwise than by ordinary sight', especially, it goes on to say, 'of a prophetic or mystical character, or having the nature of a revelation'. I myself, having experienced nothing of this latter variety other than a tip for a horse that did actually run but sadly failed to win, will stick firmly to the more prosaic ideas of 'thoughts, images, or fancies'... 'seen otherwise than by ordinary sight', since I understand my eyelids to be firmly closed during slumber, or so I have been told. I would beg leave to add to the definition, however, again only from my own personal observation, elements of dialogue and even of plot, as well as taking into account a childlike and virtually unassailable 'suspension of disbelief' when subjected to the sleep-bound spell of the unlikeliest of tall stories. This refreshing freedom of expression enjoyed by the unconscious mind has been with us down the centuries of course and has been tapped and explored in a variety of ways. I have tried in my case to act as a kind of creative reporter, recalling to the best of my ability the sequence of events, and as much as possible of the action and discourse that apparently occurred, then putting it into good order. In so doing I have followed a modus operandi of the French poet Paul Verlaine who, in a prose work—'Les Memoires d'un Veuf'—under the heading 'Quelqes-uns de Mes Reves' ('A Few of My Dreams') chose only those that he considered plausible or worth writing down in the cold light of day. In my own endeavours, I was unexpectedly, some might say supernaturally assisted by Rimbaud's long dead ami. Having attempted a translation of one of Monsieur Verlaine's dreams which included an appearance of his own late father, I was on the following night rewarded by the bizarre appearance of the Frenchman in a dream that concerned my father. The two dream stories that principally involve my father's death and burial have in

*fact been with me for a very long time, since the first
anniversary of his passing, which occurred on Saint
Patrick's night, 1970. They are, needless to say, very
personal, and I have until now only shared them with
close friends or relatives. It had been noted by one or two
of these acquaintances that my account seemed to vary
hardly at all over a period of some thirty years and I was
finally persuaded to transfer its telling from a fairly long-
established oral version to a written one.*

*The setting for my father's final resting place is
entirely fanciful, not to say far-fetched in such a
religiously divided community as our own. There may
however be some hidden psychological agenda at work
here—in my own mind, I hasten to add, not that of my
late parent. Yet it is worth recording, in tribute to both
my parents that not a trace of sectarian bigotry entered
their thinking. They chose their friends from all sections
of the community and my dear mother's avowed faith
was based on the belief that every class, colour, and creed
under heaven, along with lion, mongrel dog and "wee
sleekit, cowrin', timorous beastie", were all equally God's
bairns. As for my father, his creed followed the poet
Burns:*

Dreams

For 'a that, an' 'a that,
It's comin' yet for a' that,
That man and man the world o'er
Shall brothers be for 'a that.

The thoughts and dreams that follow are dedicated to
their memory:

We are such stuff
As dreams are made on,
and our little lifeIs rounded with a sleep ...

The Fault of Paul Verlaine
(and 'Le Chat Noir')

I shall attempt to describe in as much detail as I can some of my recurring dreams—those, naturally, which still seem of interest in the cold light of day, or that may survive re-telling in an atmosphere somewhat less plausible to the wide-awake—I ask you to bear with me; it is the fault of Paul Verlaine and comes of reading certain books rather too near bedtime. I will merely add that as he saw Paris in his subconscious mind, so I see my native city, vividly and often; yet never quite as it is in reality; that, I suppose, is the nature of dreams.

As frequently as not, it is a fractured, fragmented townscape, not unlike a cubist, or pre-cubist painting; an apparently small, yet intensely urban concept with a hard central core. It is primitive, chaotic, and encircled by a narrow river hemmed in by rows of unidentifiable trees lining either bank. Bright red brushstrokes fill gaps between the greenest of green foliage, the latter applied liberally with the palette knife; but it is the red that predominates—the red of urban brick.

By way of contrast, if I look to my left the scene is more pastoral and open, though if anything even more dream-like. A single street of kitchen houses ends abruptly as in an alfresco folk museum, and beyond it is an expansive grassy slope, a low picturesque hill surmounted by a disused brickworks with a tall, elegant chimney. Where the grass begins, a large disproportionate white rabbit is munching nonchalantly, whilst on the gable of the nearest end house a huge Ingersol pocket watch hangs from a two foot long rusty nail, its bulky silver chain draped gracefully across the space as though from a working man's waistcoat. The weather is sultry with an oppressive orange sun beating down, appropriately highlighting the equestrian portrait of Prince William of Orange that entirely covers the other end gable of this quaint little street; in the far distance there is a rhythmic throbbing of tribal drums.

I try to reconcile the two contrasting visions—the 'Surreal' and the 'Post-Impressionist'—and to rationalise my own placement in the overall picture, but in so doing I am instantly transported from the south of the city to the east of it. The images are now in black and white and quintessentially photographic though not in a literal sense; there is still, however, the barrier of water between the inner city and myself.

I am, in point of fact—if one may be allowed such an expression in the grammar of dreams—standing in the middle of a deserted suburban park, entirely surrounded by a circular river, which I intuitively know is an absurdity. I therefore check the flow and observe, as Aristotle did at Euripos, that the currents are moving both ways. The discovery does not drive me to distraction as it did the philosopher, for I know that I am standing on reclaimed land. Behind a high dyke another river flows into the sea and likely as not the two are joined in some way. Perhaps this little stream, fed from the one above, in its turn goes underground, and like Alph the sacred river, flows through caverns measureless to man—damned clever, those Dutch engineers! To return to a vaguely plausible world, however, on the far bank of the upper river are the saw-toothed rooves of workshops, the cranes and gantries of a large shipyard, and beyond that, the most impressive landmark of them all, the hill which I know from childhood to be the head of a reclining Napoleon—chin, mouth, nose, and noble brow. In the distance, on the elevated path that runs along the dyke, an elderly man comes into view walking his dog. I feel an involuntary shudder between my shoulder blades.

A small Willow Pattern bridge conveniently materializes and I step across it but remain in the selfsame park; a glance over my shoulder confirms a gut feeling that the bridge has gone. Have I been walking on water? I enter a long dark subway cut into the dyke but emerge into an identical terrain. In desperation I close my eyes for sixty seconds or so, and when I re-open them, though I am still in parkland, the surroundings and ambience are noticeably different. I approach some impressive looking wrought iron gates and walk out through them, finding myself virtually back where I had started. I look across the narrow river, and gaze once more down the little street of kitchen houses; but the Ingersol watch and chain, the white rabbit, and the brickworks with its tall chimney have all gone; only King Billy on his white horse remains, as pristine and as freshly painted as if it were yesterday. On waking it occurred to me that these images represented my earliest recollections—my first pet, my father's trusty five-shilling timepiece, and the oven that baked the bricks that built our house; but meanwhile, the dream has taken another turn.

I am suddenly caught up in a vast concourse of marching men sweeping remorselessly towards the river—banners, mace-poles, pikestaffs; flute, silver, and accordion bands; suits, sashes, and bowler hats—left right, left right, left right—then, with what can only be likened to a prolonged application of brakes, the entire procession grinds to a halt with all the awesome grandiloquence of a steam train—some lodges shunting into the ones in front, causing a certain amount of confusion and aggravation, and resulting in some instruments clattering to the ground—whilst at the front of the march there is an immediate, ugly confrontation. A steel barrier has been erected at a bridgehead where formerly—in my dream, that is—there had been no bridge. It is manned by armed police with riot shields and protective helmets. Voices are raised in anger but loud drumming drowns out the noise and counters the clamour of a protesting opposition chanting abuse from the other side of the water.

The river seemed wider now, and the whole event began to assume the nature of a crowd scene in a high budget feature film as people began drifting away from the main action to picnic in the nearby park—is that Sir Alec Guinness and Sir John Mills leaning against the railings? Was that John Wayne striding past? The wee blond scrubber screeching her lungs out is hardly Marilyn Monroe or Goldie Hawn, but she plays her role with gusto and conviction—from behind a great clump of elm trees, a hot-air balloon rises gracefully above the tumult. On it is inscribed the words: CHRIST DIED FOR THE UNGODLY. The crowd falls silent.

What now ensued was a thick, impenetrable and suffocating smog which enveloped everything and everyone, and for a while caused me to 'lose consciousness' if you follow my meaning. When I "came to" some time later, I felt distinctly dizzy and somewhat nauseous, and found that I was swinging crazily to and fro in some indeterminate limbo where I had the sensation of being buffeted by high winds. Then, as suddenly as it had arrived, the mist cleared, and I discovered that I was dangling about two hundred feet in mid-air clinging to the sides of the basket attached to the balloon I had seen take off earlier. I was still on the wrong side of the river as it were, but now I could actually see into the central area of the town. The bridge with its barrier had gone, the crowds had vanished, and the streets were deserted. In the distance were domes, church spires, a clock tower, and public buildings of various kinds, but the immediate foreground laid out before me was a tangle of mean streets—houses, backyards with washing hanging out to dry, and unseen ghostly voices echoing from ugly terraced dwellings of uniform, monotonous brick reminiscent of a vast military barracks, though more random and irregular; a claustrophobic maze of cul-de-sacs, boarded-up windows, and sinister back entries. The miserable prospect sent another shiver down my spine; an association with troubles and terror, nocturnal and other atrocities; images of bombings, blitzes, shootings and beatings; of bodies dragged from the stagnant waters of some long-forgotten canal.

Without having actually noticed, I found myself in the middle of a small, paved, pedestrianised square—except that there were no pedestrians—I must have stepped from the now deflated balloon's basket as casually as from a taxi cab. This square was entirely symmetrical with covered arcades on all four sides, unoccupied shops on the ground floor, and ghastly grey pebble-dashed flats or offices on the upper stories, likewise vacant and neglected. Desperately trying to find some sign of life, progress has become frustrating and painfully slow. My legs feel like lead weights, and as I leave one square behind and enter another, it soon becomes apparent that they are all identical and all utterly deserted. At screaming point, but lacking the strength to do so, I stand forlornly in the centre of the umpteenth unpopulated 'piazza', when out of the corner of my eye I catch a glimpse of someone or something lurking under an arch of one arcade; the creature steps out of the shadows and into the light to address me—he wears a black frock coat and top hat, white gloves and spats, and looks like a commissionaire, though he could just as easily be a tomcat. He smiles broadly, displaying a fine set of ivories—no black notes, or sharps and flats—they could be artificial or they could be his own; a splendid white keyboard just the same—a smile that my dear mother would have described as 'a basket of chips!' He speaks, but it sounds like a bar in the bass clef—

broken chords strummed with the left hand on the lower register of an old honky-tonk; I do not understand a word. He points to a nameplate at the corner of the square, then laughs—this time it sounds as though an unseen hand has run its fingernails across the entire length of his facial white notes—but the really annoying thing is, that though I studied the nameplate carefully, I cannot now for the life of me recall the name of the square. He must have taken note of my incomprehension at the time, for, again smiling from ear to ear—dare I say like a Cheshire cat—he faced me square on, and pressing a red button on his lapel, he informed me politely in a recorded voice that as I was an alien, I must report to the British Embassy and show my passport. At that he laughed quite immoderately then slunk off on all fours, his tail held high in the air!

I stood there for a while, pondering on my status as a foreigner, and wondering what to do about it. Who was he, this cool cat with the musical mouth? Where was this Embassy? Was it the building near the old railway station known as 'Headquarters' that used to proclaim to all and sundry that the province was British—a claim that was only two-thirds true—was it the travelling tally rooms in the east of the city where, for a bottle of stout and a pledge of loyalty, a working man could use his vote to land himself in the dole queue? Or was it the unemployment exchange itself? At this point, a dapper if somewhat disreputable man of uncertain years appeared in the very corner of the square through which the cat had disappeared. Leaning on a walking stick and with his right foot pointing elegantly outwards, wearing slightly flared trousers, a velvet jacket, and hat at a jaunty angle; sporting a full set of whiskers, and a thoroughly bohemian air, he smiled, and wagged an admonitory finger as though to say, 'You are taking liberties, mon ami.' Then he pointed to a sign above a door a little to his left which read 'Le Chat Noir' (The Black Cat) and, with a broad wink and a twirl of his cane, disappeared inside. This was without doubt the flamboyant lover of Arthur Rimbaud and poet of the Decadence, Monsieur Paul Verlaine whose "Memoires d'un Veuf" I had but lately read. The door through which he literally "vanished" was the entrance to the cafe which housed the press that published the magazine (all of the same name) that printed earliest verses of the avant-garde poets of his day. Such, however, is the tyranny of dreams, that I was permitted no discourse, nor enlightening dialogue. Monsieur Verlaine has said, it seems, all that Nature allows in this insubstantial world.

"We are such stuff
As dreams are made on, and our little life
Is rounded with a sleep."

The Fabric of a Dream I

Was it a vision, or a waking dream?
Fled is that music—do I wake or sleep?
            —Keats: 'Ode to a Nightingale'

Because of its exclusiveness and strict subjectivity a dream is never shared—either mentally or physically - nor can it be captured, recorded, or verified by any known agency. Though it is true to say that some dreams are less ephemeral than others, and that some are extremely vivid and eminently plausible upon waking, they tend to disperse and fade with alarming rapidity. Instant oral or written transmission, an exceptional memory, or even a fertile imagination may well preserve some fine examples of the genre for the scrutiny of the diviner or the psychoanalyst, but there is no known way of corroborating what did or did not appear in the unconscious world of another human being. A dream is by its very nature exclusive and personal, and there can be no material witnesses.

Perhaps, because of these factors, definitions tend to be, if not cautious, then decidedly basic: 'a train of thoughts, images, or fancies passing through the mind while asleep' ... 'the state in which this occurs'. The figurative definitions go little further: 'a vision of the fancy indulged in while awake' ... 'a reverie', or 'castle in the air'; whilst the literal, if archaically far-fetched explanation of a nightmare is, of all things, "a female monster", (surely not a she-horse) which attempts to suffocate, or smother its victim while asleep. Alternatively, it is simply 'a bad dream'. These are hardly heroic endeavours by the lexicographer to evoke a highly-charged and universal phenomenon that has been with us from Jacob and his miraculous ladder, Joseph and his amazing dreamcoat, to Martin Luther King's prophetic vision, and Nelson Mandela's far from idle reveries; a mystical element in the human psyche that has played a significant role in literature, music, and the visual arts, been a spur for the movers and shakers of our turbulent planet, and a safety valve and refuge for the meek and poor in spirit.

Indeed, the dream for all its elusiveness and lack of material substance, retains not only its mystery, but remains a compulsive fascination and prime source of artistic inspiration. Monsieur Verlaine, the author of a favourite bedtime book and a fleeting fellow traveller in one of my own nocturnal adventures, moves easily when recounting his own dreams from one fantastical scenario to the next with a casual "et voici bien d'une autre" (and here, then is another one), which of course is a notable characteristic of these nightly perambulations. He mentions that his father, "himself dead for some time", is a frequent companion in his dream world, and encouraged by that example, I have on impulse had the notion of introducing my own parents, though in rather a different context. In so doing, I will expose a personal superstition inherited from my immediate family and a gaggle of wily old aunts, concerning the importance of breaking a dream, which is to say that the experience is firstly recalled to the realm of conscious thought, acknowledged for what it is, and finally dispersed and sublimated. Failure to do so can result in repressed emotions, the bearing of irrational grudges, or just a general feeling of confusion and malaise. Symptoms were readily spotted by these shrewd ladies, and signs of shock or unwonted introspection often led to probing questions of what you thought you did, or where you thought you were the previous night. An irrational or patently nonsensical answer would result in the clapping of hands and demonstrations of joy and delight: "He's broken his dream," they'd cry. "The child has broken his dream!" "You were nowhere of the sort", they'd chortle, "you were safely tucked up in bed!"—no fear now of latent neuroses, of hemmed in evil spirits; no locked up demons, or monsters of the night—what sterling therapists they were, these wise old birds! As for that insipid definition, 'a bad dream', it is, to say the least, a gross understatement for my earliest, most alarming, and probably shortest cauchemar. The entire action—and you'll have to take my word for this—lasted a matter of thirty seconds or so, but the impact and its aftermath were in truth cataclysmic. The fact of the matter—if I may use that expression is that I pulled a lavatory chain just as I saw my mother's face looking up from beneath the water in the pan. She vanished round the S-bend, and despite all my efforts to dive in and save her, she did not re-appear. Waking instantly and reaching the real toilet in one mad bound, I found the water as still as a mill-pond and not a sign of mother. Becoming completely hysterical, I wept uncontrollably, and was inconsolable even after I found she and my father alive and safe in their bed!

The worst nightmare of all, of course, is the one from which we do not wake, or rather, we do, yet pain and sorrow remain—the disaster, or bereavement, the irreversible tragedy which sleep cannot annul, which does not leave with dawn's first light, or vanish with the morning dew. To each of these is a time and season, so we are led to believe; at all events they have no hiding place in dreams except as formless shadows—though shadow is cast by substance, as Dante knew full well.

In later years my father was affectionately known as 'The Man with the Dog'. This amused him in his quiet way, and if, when dressed in cap, muffler, and overcoat, anyone was foolish enough to ask him where he was going, he would reply with a rueful grin: "I'm off to mow a meadow!" "The only reason they use that daft expression", he would cheerfully add, "is because the dog is the star turn!" Indeed Rex, a shaggy black and white border collie crossed with a more square-headed terrier of some sort, was a remarkable canine athlete. Picked up by my mother and brought home after being knocked down by a trolleybus, he was lovingly nursed back to health and strength in front of our kitchen fire then slowly rehabilitated by short walks to the nearby park until fully recovered. Despite notices in local shops, and bits of paper pinned to neighbourhood trees, he was never claimed, and so to everyone's relief he became a second family pet, harmoniously sharing hearth and home with "Ginger", an urbane marmalade tom cat who had a short but distinguished acting career, appearing in 'Bell Book and Candle' and 'The Diary of Ann Frank' at the Empire, and Group theatres, back in the good old days.

Over the years, under the patient guidance of my father, the dog's sporting skills, especially with a pliant and a lively rubber ball (much chewed), developed to a remarkable degree. Bounced off the sloping bank of a long dyke, and rebounding at crazy, unpredictable angles, or ricocheting off the rooves of low pavilions in the Park, Rex never took his eye off that ball and seldom missed a catch, however difficult. On the rare occasion that he did, the hang-dog look of self-disgust matched that of any sporting prima donna who has missed an open goal or fumbled a chance in the slips.

I have a 'vignette' of Rex in action which is locked

away in my memory, and has not faded with time. I can call it to mind as readily as if it were on video. It is, however, inevitably followed by, and is, in a curious way inseparable from a more disturbing set of images which lie dormant for long periods, but which when re-awakened, also display remarkable durability, consistency and clarity. These 'pictures' are more random and inconsequential, resembling in that sense a silent movie, though there is some dialogue. The whole scenario goes back in time some thirty years and more, but I shall endeavour to recall it faithfully. In fact—once more taking a leaf out of that book of Monsieur Verlaine, who had a not entirely dissimilar experience—I undertake to describe it "aussi minutieusement que possible"—as precisely as I possibly can.

The action begins without preamble. Rex has returned the ball and is poised for the next throw. My father has the ball in his right hand and is gazing down fondly at his faithful hound whose eyes flit between my father's face and hand with intense concentration. There is a perfect bond between man and dog, every bit as serious as though it were a matter of life and death, as it often can be if the man has a gun in his hand. I was standing right behind them but cannot remember whether we had set out together or I had caught them up in order to surprise them, as I often did when home on a visit; in any event I was a mere spectator. My father threw the ball—though rather frail now he still had a good arm—and it sailed through the air aimed to strike near the top of the sloping bank. Just as it left his hand I caught sight of another dog setting off at speed—a menacing mongrel of mixed ancestry, something between a pit bull terrier and a rottweiler, and built like a concrete-mixer—the two animals were on a collision course. As Rex rose onward and upward to meet the awkward bounce it instantly became apparent that the rival animal was second best, but without wavering or breaking stride, the beast rammed our dog amidships causing him to yelp with pain; it was a blatant foul! The "concrete-mixer" plunged unceremoniously into the dyke, but Rex seemed to hover in mid-air for a moment. The ball must have hit a stone or piece of rock for it had come off at a higher trajectory than usual and was spinning backwards. Rex caught sight of it and turned over in flight like a high diver, sailing over the prostrate 'Pit-Rottweiler' belly upwards, and catching the missile in his gaping jaws before landing heavily and awkwardly on his back, then rolling down the slope and lying deadly still. "He's broken his back," I heard my father say, as he stood for a moment rooted to the spot. Happily, such was not the case. Slowly and painfully, Rex got back on all fours, obviously winded from when his opposite number had knocked the stuffing out of him, but triumphant nonetheless. He limped back, head down but tail wagging, and placed the ball at his master's feet. As he crouched down to congratulate and comfort the dog I heard father say, "Agh, that's it boy, that's enough for the day, you're done in; we're both done in." He struggled to rise but shrugged off my attempt to help him to his feet as he thrust himself upward on both legs with an audible constriction of the breath. He smiled his rueful smile and simply said, "I'm done for son, and that's a fact."

That, so to speak, concludes the 'video'—had they been around at the time I might have caught that particular vignette or something similar on a camcorder—but the set of jerky lantern slides that follow it obey a different set of rules entirely. Not nearly as palpable or credible in retrospect, I remember that they made a crazy kind of sense at the time. Surreal, shocking, hypnotic, and sometimes spellbinding on the one hand, commonplace and even vaguely plausible on the other, they called to mind that dubious truism, 'Seeing is believing'.

Father for some reason had opted for the long way home, staying on the wrong side of the railway tracks and ending up at the road bridge near a main entrance to the shipyard. He looked wistfully at the place where he had toiled for so many years, then turned to walk away. After a hundred yards or so he paused; the rise and fall of the bridge made him suddenly breathless again and he sat down on the low wall of a pebble-dashed mission hall to rest. The wayside pulpit read 'Come unto me all ye that labour', and so on. Across the street was a row of nondescript shops among which was a small neighbourhood chemist. I suggested calling in, and father rose wearily to cross the road. Telling the dog to "stay", and gesturing for me to keep an eye on him, he went inside.

The dog was literally at the end of his tether, and flung himself down full-length on the pavement, with his muzzle between his front paws. I lit a cigarette and looked up and down the familiar street, which seemed strange all of a sudden. Across the road, the wayside pulpit now read 'Vote Labour', and the kerb edges were painted red, white, and blue—something I had not noticed previously. Looking to my left, an empty hearse appeared from over the bridge and came to a halt about three doors away; the driver got out and walked into one of the shops. I glanced over my shoulder and the chemist's was now a doctor's surgery, or rather a waiting room. I checked next door to see if I had shifted my position, but the dog had certainly not stirred. It was the same door my father had walked through. I entered and looked around, but though there were seats against the walls, the room was uninhabited. Through a half open door I caught sight of my father sitting on a chair with his shirt unbuttoned down the front. A doctor of about my own age emerged, closing the door behind him. "Are you his son?" he enquired. I nodded. "I'm afraid I have some rather bad news for you," he said gravely. "Your father is dead." I opened my mouth in disbelief, but the doctor pressed on, "Clinically dead, that is, meaning that ensuing symptoms are merely a completion of that condition and are irreversible. I suggest you get him home fairly quickly, though there are of course some formalities." Again I opened my mouth to speak, but the doctor ploughed on: "I've told him and he has taken it quite well; we think it best under the circumstances. His only worry seems to be how to break it to his wife, but I'm sure you can ... mumble, mumble."

After that, everything seemed to happen incredibly quickly, but a bizarre kind of logic swept me along with events. My father's apologetic face nearly tore my heart out. He had been a perfect gentleman all his life and even in extremis he did not want to cause inconvenience. I put my arms around him as he was about to attend to his still sleeping dog, but a smiling business-like receptionist claimed his attention. "Would you care to step this way sir?" she said brightly, opening a hitherto unobserved door in the right hand wall—a sliding door in fact—and ushering my father through. It led to premises next door, which turned out to be a bespoke tailor. My father was shown all sorts of dark suiting cloths, but was thoroughly at a loss without my mother on hand to advise; and besides, he had never worn anything but ready made. "Perhaps a plain navy blue serge sir—the clerical grey is a little too sombre don't you think?"

The Fabric of a Dream I

My father nodded politely and that was that—navy blue serge it was—"excellent choice if I may say so, sir, and very hard-wearing." Dad could not resist a smile at this, but it went unnoticed. In no time, a tape measure had been run over him, a sleeveless jacket with white tacking-stitching had been removed from the dummy, tried for size, and marked with tailor's chalk before being replaced with the finished article— presumably one they had made earlier—a shirt and sober tie were offered for inspection, and presently he emerged from a changing cubicle dressed to kill! In the adjoining room further along he was given a trim, a shave, and a quick makeover that left him looking as pale as death, and further along still, we were shown into the carpentry department where my father admired some nice looking timber stacked against one wall—oak, elm, beech and mahogany—whilst against an adjacent wall, half a dozen coffins stood in line like a ghoulish identity parade. A suitably obsequious individual tried to play things down a little. "I think this is a bit too pale and mournful. The mahogany is very dignified but it's also more warm and cheerful. The one in the corner looks about right for size— would you care to step inside sir? ..." I am nearing breaking point here and decide it is time to wake up. I go outside for a breath of fresh air and inhale deeply for a spell. I pinch myself quite viciously in the upper arm, emitting a loud cry of pain as I do so, then jump up and down on the spot several times yelling at the top of my voice, "Wake up! Wake up! Wake up!" It is all to no avail, but a small crowd has gathered across the street to observe my antics. I just cannot bear the thought of my father standing in that upright casket like some fossilised sentry from some long forgotten fort, when all my rational being is bristling with disbelief. Just then he emerges from the building accompanied by the undertaker, who hands me the keys of the hearse and indicates that I should drive. The tailor approaches with a bag containing dad's 'civvy' clothes, and hands me a long envelope which I take to be a bill—he has also acquired a new overcoat, hat, and gloves by the way, and is looking very smart—finally the doctor's receptionist hurries out with another long envelope which I imagine is a certificate stating the cause of death. As we drive away, my father smiles and waves, then suddenly realises that we have forgotten the dog. I apply the brakes and wind down the window. There is Rex, who had obviously risen from his slumber and been trotting along behind us. He refused to get in the vehicle but galloped on ahead, and was on the doorstep when we arrived home. We sat in the car for a while wondering what to do next, but soon realised we had been accompanied when we saw an undertaker's man walk up the path and ring the front doorbell. My sister answered the door—mother was poorly and in bed at the time—and two more men carried a casket and trestles up the hallway and into the front room; the dog had disappeared. I helped my father out of the car and into the house. He hung his new overcoat and hat carefully on the hallstand, tucking the gloves in a side pocket. I heard my mother's voice call out "Is that you love?" and he replied, "Yes, dear." "Break it to her gently son," he said. "I feel my joints stiffening up, so I had better familiarise myself with the sentry box"; and with that he went in to the parlour and closed the door.

There are gaps and empty spaces in my memory here—whether of reality or dream I know not which—though of what remains, long dead ancestral visitors mingling with living mourners belong in the latter world, whilst my father's actual presence in the house, and my mother's tangible grief belong to the former. The remaining 'Dream narrative' which is indelibly engraved on my subconscious mind, and which surfaces from time to time with remarkable consistency of detail and clarity of recall, has to a certain extent blurred my recollection of the actual events, though of course I can still distinguish between the two. Perhaps a metaphor for this distinction may be found in expressionist art where a finished work is likely to be more emphatic, and is certainly designed to outlive the emotions and subject matter that gave rise to it; the Norwegian painter Edvard Munck's 'The Scream' is a fair example I think. What is yet to be told, and I shall do so presently, is what amounts to a sequel to what I have endeavoured to describe so far. It is the second half of a moving picture show, but because of the lacunae, or blank spaces, it seems preferable to change reels and begin again. Its title will be simply 'The Fabric of a Dream II' and it will conclude the story.

The Fabric of a Dream II

If, as Lord Chesterfield has remarked, having frequent recourse to narrative betrays great want of imagination, then so be it. What follows is largely narration, in that it is an account of a sequence of events—be they real or imagined—which, when retold in good order, amounts to a story; one, moreover, that has been lodged in my unconscious, or subconscious mind for some considerable time. It is of course a continuation of the previous tale, but because it is a new beginning I will resist the temptation to look back, and allow the sequel to have a life of its own. It is not, I hasten to add, part of a recondite private journal recording a stream of random thoughts and pictures, but rather, a positive surge of dream energy released and made available to the conscious mind in a disturbing, yet ultimately therapeutic fashion, or so I have found it; a sublimation through image and metaphor of the irreversible process which we call mortality.

There is, needless to say, a gaping, not to say unbridgeable dichotomy between the waking and unconscious states, and actions are not interchangeable or necessarily compatible in these disparate worlds. Though emotional and, more rarely ,ideological vibrations may oscillate between the two, rational thought is at a distinct disadvantage in the world of dreams, despite Lamb's assertion that they are real, and that they each have "a venue in their respective districts of dreamland." Disbelief and even scepticism sometimes raise their heads in dreams it is true, but how often do those intimations of revolt return us to the material world—without, say, the intrusion of an alarm clock, or things that go bump in the night. This story, on both planes—the real and the imaginary is motivated by the same occurrence, namely my father's funeral, and though it is the latter version that over the years has proved more durable both in detail and clarity, I shall try to recall what memories that remain of the day itself, in the cold light of reality, and with as little embellishment as flawed recollection allows. It is a daunting task, though one or two mental pictures are already coming into focus.

The Fabric of a Dream II

There was, of course, my father's brooding presence in the front room, which I had come to accept as I ushered visitors in and out. I read into his unchanging expression, notes of acceptance, of calm resignation, and even of passive expectation, something I had observed in a theatre once, as we waited for the lights to dim. On that occasion his face had lit up like a child's at the rise of the curtain, and I accepted there and then with the utmost sadness that it would never do so again in this world. My first task that morning had been to attend to my mother. She was at that time very frail and on the doctor's insistence she had so far remained in bed. As I entered the room she was serenely asleep and I was reluctant to wake her, but she must have sensed my presence. Grasping at straws, she said: "It's not a dream, is it son?" and an expression of infinite sadness returned to her face, a look which never quite left her while she lived; for she loved him dearly, as he had loved her. I was privileged to be told something of that love when it was new and in its prime, how it had blossomed, and how it had endured; warming and gladdening the family home in good times and in bad. How she took her farewell a short time later when I had carried her downstairs is a scene too harrowing to relate, and I am glad I was the only witness of it. Suffice to say that it had all the dignity and pathos of a woman in extremis, and despite her firm faith and unshakeable Christian belief, something of the pagan passion of an ancient Greek tragedy.

The formalities followed in due order. An informal service which drifted back and forth from parlour to kitchen, was conducted by two pastors, or ministers— one a breakaway, or rather Free Methodist from just across the road, and the other a Seventh Day Adventist from the other side of town. My mother and sister, and one or two nieces seemed happy with this arrangement, though several relations were, to say the least, a little puzzled; one elderly cousin formed the opinion that the two men seemed at times to vie or contend for the soul of the departed and was heard to mutter audibly, "What's going on here?" while a Catholic auntie discreetly made the sign of the cross and mouthed her own silent aspirations. Soon afterwards the undertaker's men entered the house, and after the lid of the coffin had been screwed down, it was deftly removed and placed in position behind the hearse. In Ireland in those days the women did not attend the actual burial, but stayed behind to comfort the widow and prepare a cold repast for the returning mourners, so with sorting out cars and organising bearers for the 'carry', I have very little memory of the departure, though I do recall many faces, mostly women's, standing at doors on either side of the street. As we turned into the main road and halted to install the casket in the funeral car, I was astonished to find that a sizeable body of men had fallen in behind the cortege. I shook hands with many of them and found they were mainly old shipyard colleagues who had come to pay their respects.

The interment itself was a bleak and joyless affair. I remember the open grave and the pile of earth—the "Dust to dust" and the "Sure and certain hope"; the rattle of damp sods on the coffin lid, and the waiting gravediggers leaning on Lurgan spades—and inwardly wondering if there wasn't a better way. For the journey back, having seen friends and relations into cars, I was not in the mood for small talk and opted for a lift in the empty hearse; it seemed more impersonal somehow, and I could organise my brain for the well-deserved gratuities and thanks—they had been wonderful. The older man sat in the middle, and the younger one was driving. I gazed out of the window for a while and they left me alone with my thoughts. When after several minutes I began to express my gratitude, the driver asked what I had thought of my father. I replied that I thought the world of him, and there was an awkward pause as a look was exchanged between the two men. The older man tried to explain: "He means, what did you think of him? What did you think of his ..." he broke off, embarrassed, as the young man's face started to turn pink. Only then did I realise. He wanted to know what I had thought of his handiwork, how my father had looked in his coffin. To this day I am touched by that pride in a job that many find macabre, and I told him so at the time.

The aftermath at the house was painful and long drawn out, made more so by my mother's bravery and the want of a comforting drink; we were a temperance household and it would have been unthinkable to have flaunted the custom now. One or two relations however were secret tipplers in that covert Presbyterian manner which has lent the very name to the side door of Ulster pubs. None of the men broke ranks, but by early evening, when my mother was plainly exhausted, a forthright female cousin and favourite of my father, saw her into bed with hot water bottle, warm drink and sedative. The two women had reached an accommodation, for sweeping majestically downstairs, Lily announced to one and all that her taxi was arriving and that I was seeing her home. "Go upstairs and see your mother now", said she, "and when you come down everyone can say their goodnights." A visit to the bedroom confirmed what I had guessed, "Go with your cousin Lily and I'll see you in the morning", said my mother. "Another cousin is staying the night and you'll only be in the way; good-night son, and God bless."

"I'm taking you to a wee snug I know on my side of town", said cousin Lily as the taxi sped away. "You'll know it when you get there, for you've been in once or twice, I'm told; and it's there we'll wish your father 'God speed', and tell old tales, and sing his favourite songs, and truly honour his memory."

*　*　*　*　*　*

I like to think that the dreams I had that night were benign and compassionate but I have no memory of them. The visions that remain with me first appeared almost one year later, not on the anniversary of the funeral, but exactly twelve months after the actual date of his death, which was Saint Patrick's Day, the 17th March; and the story that they tell is the completion of the narrative that ended part one of this tale—what I have already called 'The second half of a moving picture show.'

It is a bright, slightly windy March day, with broad patches of clear blue sky and I am taking my father for a drive. It is a carefree, country-outing kind of jaunt without any pressing awareness of time or destination. The Mourne Mountains are mentioned, or even perhaps glimpsed in the distance, and a passing reference to a beauty spot there called the Silent Valley seems suddenly to appeal to the old man's sense of the ridiculous—"Good name for a graveyard, eh?" This comment cuts into the carefree mood, and triggers half-forgotten mental pictures from elsewhere in this sequence. I notice, for instance, how very well-dressed my father is, and seem to recall a visit to a tailor. Come to think of it, I too am rather well turned out— where can we be bound for? The countryside has noticeably altered, with orchards and shuttered farms. Could this be northern France? Are we in Normandy?

The Fabric of a Dream II

No scathing voice mocks the question. No rational thought queries its validity—seeing is indeed believing—it looks like Normandy, ergo it is Normandy! We have just entered a pale town that's been painted by Utrillo in his White Period—'Paysage de Banlieue' or 'Suburban Landscape'—we pass some modest gates on our left and drive down a narrow street, turning right at the bottom, when suddenly much larger gates confront us, leading into a kind of park.

There are four stout, ornate stone gateposts, two on each side of a wide carriage entrance, with pedestrian access to left and right. Surmounting these posts—four elaborate lamps or lanterns topped by silver crosses and having six or eight glazed panels intricately mounted and chased. Wrought iron gates are open wide, and beyond, set into a grassy terraced hill, is a broad flight of ceremonial steps with six or seven terraces; at the summit, a massive, pale grey Gothic cathedral.

I have driven through the gates and drawn to a standstill. One or two people are strolling about at the foot of the steps and some few are ascending. Others are attempting to take a broad, gently sloping path to the left, which strikes me as an easier way up to the plateau than the formidable stone stairway. I particularly noted that this path bore to the left, and that there was no equivalent access to the right. My father and I sat there quietly for some time admiring the impressive facade, which is why its salient features are so firmly imprinted upon my mind. Two sturdy towers topped by chunky spires rising to two hundred feet or so, one with a clock face just below the belfry. At their base two stout wooden doors with carved stone hoods in the Perpendicular style, so that the horizontal heads are aligned with the base of the windows immediately above, forming an architectural unit. Above this level, the style appeared to alter—the great west window and those of the belfry being of an earlier order of Gothic—which struck me as being the wrong way round—was I dreaming? Across the front of the nave, was a canopied gallery of sculpted statues each in its separate niche—twelve in all; or was it eleven?—surely the apostles; and directly below these figures, was the west door.

Such was the hypnotic effect of the spectacle before us, that I found myself in a sort of reverie or brown study, a heavy-lidded or soporific sensation almost causing me to nod off, when, blinking consciously to stop this occurring, I caught sight of some once familiar figures on the top level—an aunt and two uncles that I knew for certain were long dead—I felt a numbing chill at the base of my spine! At that moment, cousin Lily appeared out of the blue wearing a satin turquoise costume with matching pillbox hat, and pinned white carnations to our lapels. Mouthing "God speed" and muttering under her breath something about not being able to stay, as it wasn't her sort of place, she dabbed her eyes with a lace handkerchief, and jumped into a waiting taxi. Father was still smiling serenely, but hearing some movement behind us and catching a glimpse of black frock coat I became aware that I was sitting behind the wheel of the dreaded hearse. Doors were opened for us, and as my father and I stepped out we were ushered towards the gently sloping path. Glancing back I saw a coffin already balanced on the shoulders of formally dressed bearers, and looking up, saw to my astonishment what looked like cardinals in full regalia waiting to receive it—two on each terrace, making fourteen in all! A sacristan had emerged from a little lodge to the left of the gates, and motioned us to commence walking up the hill just as the cortege began its long, stately climb up the ceremonial stairway.

Despite the gentle slope, my father's breathing was laboured, but we kept a steady pace and entered the church by the north transept in ample time, being shown to our seats on the left of the centre aisle of the great nave. Looking across we caught sight of my sister and my mother who smiled wanly and waved. My father smiled back apologetically as though to say "I'm sorry to be the cause of all this fuss." Other relations and friends amounting to several dozen, were on that side though I knew for a fact that many of them were no longer of this world. It didn't seem to bother my father, who pointed out who they were and waved in recognition, but I felt uneasy and embarrassed. The nave was packed to capacity, but as far as I could make out, the majority were strangers. All at once the great door swung open, a fanfare of trumpets sounded, and as the cortege, flanked by the cardinals entered the cathedral, the vast congregation rose to its feet. Only my father and myself remained seated.

What followed, or appeared to follow, seems almost too far-fetched to relate, though neither I nor my father seemed to have any problems with what was occurring, as a fairly flamboyant ceremonial reached its spectacular climax and, to us, quite plausible conclusion. In retrospect however, I am fully persuaded that what 'took place'—or 'appeared to"'take place—was a surreal, highly subjective, wildly inaccurate impression of a full scale requiem, punctuated by incongruous and wholly inappropriate inconsistencies, some of which should have beggared belief—as for example when the Salvation Army mingled with the mourners rattling their own collection boxes and brandishing copies of *The War Cry*, or the moment when an entire row of Orangemen wearing their sashes crept out apologetically, concluding correctly that they were in the wrong place at the wrong time.

These anachronistic ecumenical anomalies apart, what happened next was the placing of the casket on a kind of trolley which ran on specially laid tracks designed to protect the mosaic floor of the aisle. It came to rest just a few feet in front of where we were seated, for reasons that would later become apparent; I noticed that it had a footplate and handrail at its rear. Simultaneously, what turned out to be the officiating prelate—an athletic and rather theatrical priest in black vestments—descended from a canopied, magnificently carved marble pulpit to greet the cortege, and from the epistle side of the altar steps began to intone the Introit: "Requiem aeternam ..." and so on, which was clearly comprehended as 'Eternal rest give unto them, O Lord, and let perpetual light shine upon them.' Father nodded his approval. This in turn modulated to the Greek 'Kyrie Eleison'—'Lord have mercy upon us'—which was blasted out in triplicate by an unseen choir concealed behind a majestic, five-bayed rood screen of carved marble, with a finely sculpted Crucifixion dominating the central arch above the altar, before which the priest now stood. Directly behind him, the tabernacle housing the sacrament is correctly draped with a purple veil.

So far, so good, but now things begin to fall apart again, to smudge, and to blur. A sudden burst of the Hallelujah Chorus noisily intrudes, though my father seems to enjoy this—merrily joining in—but when the Amen Chorus drowns it out, he decides to 'take the mickey' by singing 'The Song of the Flea' at the top of his voice! In a bubble of tranquillity he quite unexpectedly appeared at the front of the congregation and sang quite beautifully in his rich baritone voice 'Ora Pro Nobis', which he sometimes did at home at the request of my Catholic Auntie Lizzie. I caught a glimpse of her sitting by my mother, both ladies looking proud and serene. It was to be his swansong, for towards its close I saw, to my horror, other coffins moving along the rails from the back of the nave, clumsily shunting into each other as they ground to a halt despite the efforts of their attendants to maintain dignity. Some wreaths and other floral tributes slid off the coffin lids giving rise to distress among a number of women who began to weep audibly. Father was unceremoniously hustled back to his seat as his personal 'trolley' was moved back into place. At the top of the altar steps, the priest turned dramatically to face the congregation holding high above his head a huge silver salver, as though showing the monstrance containing the Host to the people. He turned first to the left, then to the right, and finally out front again, and each movement was greeted with an involuntary aspiration of "Lord have mercy ..." or something similar. Attached to this salver, and miraculously adhering to it despite the elevation, was an enormous heart shaped biscuit resembling shortbread, and in its core or centre, a large, jewel-like, bright red decoration, which could have been a garnet, or a king-sized glacé cherry. The priest then swept hurriedly down the aisle and thrust the object right in my father's face. He simply nodded, and with that the cleric produced a small but lethal looking silver hammer and smashed the great biscuit to smithereens, immediately holding it up for all to see and proclaiming with histrionic flair, "Now cracks a noble heart!" The shattered fragments still clung to the salver as little rivulets of what looked like blood ran between the crevices giving an artist's impression of a massive coronary. Father's head simply sagged, or subsided onto his chest. Without further ado, and with no chance to say good-bye, he was assisted in a trance-like state onto the trolley where his hands were seen to grip the handrail. The entire Ghost Train lurched forward with alternate carriages in turn disappearing through ornate arches on either side of the reredos, my father's trolley opting for the left one. It was all over in a matter of minutes, and I was left standing in the middle of the empty nave. The clergy had vanished as had the congregation, nor was there

any sign of my mother, my sister, or any other friends
or relations. I walked to the door and gazed out over
what I was sure was a continental townscape. Looking
down the great flight of steps I saw a familiar looking
black and white mongrel struggling up from the last
but one terrace. His paws were bloodied and he
looked completely done for. I crouched down to
comfort him, but with a scarcely audible whimper he
avoided me and entered the empty cathedral, heading
straight for the high altar. It was Rex. He hesitated at
the foot of the altar steps, and slipped clumsily,
appearing almost to genuflect, before choosing the
same arch as his master.

It was a great many years before I finally put that
dream to rest. The details have remained remarkably
consistent for a very long time, and to one or two
close friends I have related the story orally, as one
would naturally have done by a warm turf fire in days
gone by. Yet the fact remained that I could never
assign to it a local habitation and a name. I was
convinced for a while that the great church, or at least
something resembling it, belonged somewhere in
Normandy or thereabouts, and looked with some
curiosity at Caen, Coutances, Evreux, and several

other possible venues, but none of them were in anything like the right setting, so I finally accepted that the whole thing, architectural details included, were a figment of my fertile imagination. Then one day, not so very long ago, I stepped out of the Beresford Arms in the city of Armagh, and though I intended to turn left, because there were some hefty roadworks in my way, I turned right on impulse and after walking down English Street, passing the junction with Dawson Street, and bearing left round the Shambles Market, I found myself in Cathedral Road. I came to a break in a stone wall and there it was—gateposts with ornamental lamps, the seven-tiered ceremonial steps, the pathway to the left, and up on the hill the great Neo-Gothic Cathedral itself! I was completely bowled over, and on recovering my composure, decided to piece together the entire dream experience. The exterior—steps, path, facade with the two styles of Perpendicular and Decorated, the twin spires and the clock, the gallery of apostles, were all there. Inside was familiar, yet somehow a disappointment. Where were the carved altar and great marble pulpit? Where was the magnificent rood screen with its sculpted Crucifixion, and its finely chiselled flanking arches? My mind was swiftly put at ease by a local informant. These had been removed on the instructions of the Second Vatican Council for reasons which do not concern my story, but I was shown pictures of them; some of the workmanship has been preserved it seems, and transferred to the nearby Saint Patrick's Church at Kilmore. So there you have it! The temporal structure may have altered slightly, but my dream fabric is still in place—if anything, more securely than ever.